Time's Arrow

By the same author

The Rachel Papers
Dead Babies
Success
Other People: A Mystery Story
Money
Einstein's Monsters
London Fields

————

Journalism

Invasion of the Space Invaders
The Moronic Inferno and Other Visits to America

Time's Arrow

or

The Nature of the Offense

Martin Amis

Harmony Books   New York

Published by Harmony Books, a division of Crown Publishers, Inc.,
201 East 50th Street, New York, New York 10022. Member of
the Crown Publishing Group.
Published in Great Britain by Jonathan Cape Limited in 1991.

Harmony and colophon are trademarks of Crown Publishers, Inc.

Manufactured in the United States of America

Library of Congress Cataloging-in-Publication Data

Amis, Martin.
Time's arrow / Martin Amis.—1st ed.
p.   cm.
I. Title.
PR6051.M5T5   1991
823'.914—dc20   91-4144
CIP

ISBN 0-517-58515-4
10   9   8   7   6   5   4   3   2   1
First American Edition

to Sally

Contents

Part I

Part II

Part III

Part I

1
___

What goes around comes around

I moved forward, out of the blackest

sleep, to find myself surrounded by

doctors . . . American doctors:

I sensed their vigor, scarcely held in check, like the profusion of their body hair; and the forbidding touch of their forbidding hands—doctor's hands, so strong, so clean, so aromatic. Although my paralysis was pretty well complete, I did find that I could move my eyes. At any rate, my eyes moved. The doctors seemed to be availing themselves of my immobility. They were, I sensed, discussing my case, but also other matters having to do with their copious free time: hobbies, and so on. And the thought came to me, surprising in its fluency and confidence, fully formed, fully settled: How I hate doctors. Any doctors. All doctors. Consider the Jewish joke, with the old lady running distractedly along the seashore: *Help! My son the doctor is drowning*. Amusing, I suppose. Her pride, I suppose, is amusing: it is greater than her love. But why the pride in these *doctor* children (why not shame, why not incredulous dread?): intimates of bacilli and trichinae, of trauma and mortification, with their disgusting vocabulary and their disgusting furniture (the bloodstained rubber bib, hanging on its hook). They are life's gatekeepers. And why would anyone want to be that?

The doctors around my bed were, of course, in leisurewear; they sent off a fuzz of suntanned self-possession, together with the unanimity that comes from safety in numbers. Given my circumstances, I might have found their manner insultingly casual. Yet I was reassured by the very vapidity of these doctors or joggers or bodybuilders, these vigor-experts—something to do with their unsmiling pursuit of the good life. The good life, at least, is better than the bad life. It features windsurfing, for example, and sweet deals in futures, and archery, and hang gliding, and fine dining. In my sleep I had dreamed of a . . . No, it wasn't like that. Let me put it this way: presiding over the darkness out of which I had loomed there was a figure, a male shape, with

4

an entirely unmanageable aura, containing such things as beauty, terror, love, filth, and above all power. This male shape or essence seemed to be wearing a white coat (a medic's stark white smock). And black boots. And a certain kind of smile. I think the image might have been a ghost-negative of doctor number one—his black tracksuit and power-pack plimsolls, and the satisfied wince he gave as he pointed at my chest with a shake of his head.

Time now passed untrackably, for it was given over to struggle, with the bed like a trap or a pit, covered in nets, and the sense of starting out on a terrible journey, toward a terrible secret. What did the secret have to do with? Him, with him: the worst man in the worst place at the worst time. I was definitely becoming stronger. My doctors came and went, with heavy hands and heavy breath, to admire my new gurgles and whimpers, my more spectacular twitches, my athletic jolts. Often, a nurse was there, alone, in adorable vigil. Her cream uniform made a packety sound—a sound in which, I felt, I could repose all my yearning and my trust. Because by this stage I was remarkably improved, feeling really tip-top. Never better. Sensation and all its luxuries returned first to my left side (suddenly) and then to my right (with gorgeous stealth). I even won praise from the nurse by lithely arching my back, more or less unassisted, when she did her thing with the pan. . . . Anyway, I lay there, in a mood of quiet celebration, for however long it was, until the evil hour—and the orderlies. The golfing doctors I could handle, the nurse was an unqualified plus. But then came the orderlies, who dealt with me by means of electricity and air. There were three of them. They were unceremonious. They hurried into the room and bundled me into my clothes and stretchered me into the garden. That's right. Then with the jump leads, like two telephones (white—white-hot), they zapped my chest. Finally, before they went away, one of them kissed me. I think I know the name of this kiss. It is called the kiss of life. Then I must have blacked out.

And when I came to it was with an audible pop in the ears, and a rich consciousness of solitude, and a feeling of love and admiration for this big stolid body I was in, which even now was preoccupied and unconcerned, straining out over the rose bed to adjust a loose swathe of clematis on the wooden wall. The big body pottered on, with slow competence: yes, it really knows its stuff. I kept wanting to relax and take a good look at the garden—but something isn't quite working. Something isn't quite working: this body I'm in won't take orders from this will of mine. Look around, I say. But his neck ignores me. His eyes have their own agenda. Is it serious? Are we okay? I didn't panic. I made do with peripheral vision, which, after all, is the next best thing. I saw curled flora swooping and trembling, like pulses or soft explosions in the side of the head. And a circumambient pale green, barred and embossed with pale light, like . . . like American money. I pottered on out there until it began to get dark. I dumped the tools in the hut. Wait a minute. Why am I walking *backward* into the house? Wait. Is it dusk coming, or is it dawn? What is the—what is the sequence of the journey I'm on? What are its rules? Why are the birds singing so strangely? Where am I heading?

A routine, in any event, has certainly established itself. It seems I'm getting the hang of things.

I live, out here, in washing-line and mailbox America, innocuous America, in affable, melting-pot, primary-color, You're-okay-I'm-okay *America*. My name, of course, is Tod Friendly. Tod *T.* Friendly. Oh, I'm there, I'm there in Salad Days, or outside Hank's Hardware World or on the patch of grass by the white town hall, with my chest thrust out and hands on hips and a kind of silent ho-ho-ho. Because that's the kind of guy I am. I'm there—I'm there at the produce store, at the post office, with my "Hi" and my "Bye now" and my "Good. Good." But it doesn't quite go like that. It goes like this:

"Dug. Dug," says the lady in the pharmacy.

"Dug," I join in. "Oo y'rrah?"

"Aid ut oo y'rrah?"

"Mh-mm," she'll say, as she unwraps my hair lotion. I walk away, backward, with a touch of the hat. I speak without volition, in the same way that I do everything else. To tell the truth, it took me quite a while to realize that the pitiable chirruping I heard all about me was, in fact, human speech. Christ, even the larks and the sparrows sound more dignified. I translate this human warble, out of interest. I soon picked it up. I know I'm fluent, now, because I can dream in it. There's another language, a second language, here in Tod's head. We sometimes dream in that language too.

But, yes, here we go, trimly hatted, finely shod, with the *Gazette* tucked under the arm, past the little driveways (THICKLY SETTLED), the lettered mailboxes (Wells, Cohen, Rezika, Meleagrou, Klodzinski, Schering-Kahlbaum, and I don't know what-all), the quiet ambition of every homestead (Please Respect Owner's Rights), the kid-filled buses and the yellow sign saying SLOW—CHILDREN and the black shape of that precipitate youngster with his clutched schoolbag (of course he's not looking. He's busy running. The face, the eyes, are downward slanted. He has no mind for cars: only for the rightful exercise of his earthly powers). When the little ones squeeze past me in the Superette, I give their mops the chaste old tousle. Tod Friendly. I have no access to his thoughts—but I am awash with his emotions. I am like a crocodile in the thick river of his feeling tone. And you know what? Each glance, each pair of eyes, even as they narrow in ingenuous appraisal, draws a bead on something inside him, and I sense the heat of fear and shame. Is that what I'm heading toward? And Tod's fear, when I stop and analyze it, really *is* frightening. And inexplicable. It has to do with his own mutilation. Who might commit it? How can he avert it?

Watch. We're getting younger. We are. We're getting stronger. We're even getting *taller*. I don't quite recognize this world we're in. Everything is familiar but not at all reassuring. Far from it. This is a world of mistakes, of diametrical mistakes. All the other people are getting younger too, but they don't seem to mind, any more than Tod minds. They don't find it counterintuitive, and faintly disgusting, as I do. Still, I'm powerless, and can do nothing about anything. I can't make myself an exception. The other people, do they have someone else inside them, passenger or parasite, like me? They're lucky. I bet they don't have the dream we have. The figure in the white coat and the black boots. In his wake, a blizzard of wind and sleet, like a storm of human souls.

Each day, when Tod and I are done with the *Gazette*, we take it back to the store. I have a good look at the dateline. And it goes like this. After October 2, you get October 1. After October 1, you get September 30. How do you figure *that?* . . . The mad are said to keep a film or stage set in their heads, which they order and art-decorate and move through. But Tod is sane, apparently, and his world is shared. It just seems to me that the film is running backward.

I'm not a complete innocent.

For instance, I find I am equipped with a fair amount of value-free information, or general knowledge, if you prefer.

$E = mc^2$. The speed of light is 186,000 miles per second. It ain't slow. The universe is finite yet boundless. As for the planets, it's Mercury, Venus, Earth, Mars, Jupiter, Saturn, Uranus, Neptune, Pluto—poor Pluto, subzero, subnormal, made of ice and rock, and so far away from the warmth and the shine. Life is no bowl of cherries. It's swings and roundabouts. You win some, you lose some. It evens out. It measures up. What goes around comes around. 1066, 1789, 1945. I have a superb vocabulary (monad, retractile, necropolis, palindrome, antidisestablishmentarianism) and a nonchalant command of all grammatical rules. The apostrophe in "Please Respect Owner's Rights" isn't where it ought to be. (Nor is the one in the placard on Route 6 that locates and praises "Rogers' Liquor Locker.") Apart from words denoting motion or process, which always have me reaching for my inverted commas ("give," "fall," "eat," "defecate"), the written language makes plain sense, unlike the spoken. Here's another joke: "She calls me up and says, 'Get over here. There's nobody home.' So I get over there, and guess what. There's nobody home." Mars is the Roman god of war. Narcissus fell in love with his own reflection—with his own soul. If you ever close a deal with the devil, and he wants to take something from you in return—don't let him take your mirror. Not your mirror, which is your reflection, which is your double, which is your secret sharer. The devil has something to be said for him: he acts on his own initiative, and isn't just following orders.

No one could accuse Tod Friendly of being in love with his own reflection. On the contrary, he can't stand the sight of it. He grooms himself by touch: he favors an electric razor and does his own barbering with a brutal pair of kitchen scissors. God knows what he looks like. There are several mirrors in our house, as you would expect, but he never confronts or consults them. I get the occasional hint from a darkened store window; sometimes, also, a chance distortion in the burnish of a faucet, of a knife. It has to be said that my curiosity is heavily qualified by trepidation. His body is not all that promising: the epic blemishes on the back of the hands, the torso loosely robed in flesh smelling of poultry and peppermint, the feet. We come across some fine old Americans in the avenues of Wellport, keglike granddads and strapping sea dogs, who are "marvelous." Tod's not marvelous. Not yet. He's still pretty wrecked, all bent and askance and ashamed. And his face? Well, it happened, one night, between bad dreams. He had inched his way to the dark bathroom, and stood slumped over the sink, feeling lost, depersonalized, and trying to soothe or tether himself with the running water. Tod moaned, and straightened before the dark mirror, and reached for the switch. Easy does it, I thought. It *would* have to happen at the speed of light. Steady now. Here goes . . .

I expected to look like shit but this was ridiculous. Jesus. We really *do* look like shit. Like a cow pat, in fact. Wow. Is there anybody genuinely around in there? Yes: slowly it took on form—Tod's head. Flanked by the great guitars of the ears, his hair lay thin over the orange-peel scalp, in white worms. Greasy, too. This I'd reckoned on: each morning he bottles the gook it gives off, and, every couple of months or so, takes it to the pharmacy for like $3.45. Ditto with the sweet-smelling powder that is shrugged out by his obscurely culpable flesh. . . . The face itself: among its ruins and relics, which say nothing, there is a swirl of expressiveness around the eyes, severe, secretive, unforgivably droll, and full of fear. Tod switched off the light. He went back to bed and resumed his nightmare. His sheets have the white smell of fear. I am obliged to smell what he smells, the baby powder, the smell of his nails

10

before the fire spits them out—to be caught in the dish and then agonizingly reapplied to his thrilled fingertips.

Is it just me, or is this a weird way to carry on? All life, for instance, all sustenance, all meaning (and a good deal of money) issue from a single household appliance: the toilet handle. At the end of the day, before my coffee, in I go. And there it is already: that humiliating *warm* smell. I lower my pants and make with the magic handle. Suddenly it's all there, complete with toilet paper, which you use and then deftly wind back on the roll. Later, you pull up your pants and wait for the pain to go away. The pain, perhaps, of the whole transaction, the whole dependency. No wonder we cry when we do it. Quick glance down at the clear water in the bowl. I don't know, but it seems to me like a hell of a way to live. Then the two cups of decaf before you hit the sack.

Eating is unattractive too. First I stack the clean plates in the dishwasher, which works okay, I guess, like all my other labor-saving devices, until some fat bastard shows up in his jumpsuit and traumatizes them with his tools. So far so good: then you select a soiled dish, collect some scraps from the garbage, and settle down for a short wait. Various items get gulped up into my mouth, and after skillful massage with tongue and teeth I transfer them to the plate for additional sculpture with knife and fork and spoon. That bit's quite therapeutic at least, unless you're having soup or something, which can be a real sentence. Next you face the laborious business of cooling, of reassembly, of storage, before the return of these foodstuffs to the Superette, where, admittedly, I am promptly and generously reimbursed for my pains. Then you tool down the aisles, with trolley or basket, returning each can and packet to its rightful place.

Another thing that seriously disappoints me about this

11

life I'm living through: the reading. I drag myself out of bed each night to start the day—and with what? Not with a book. Not even with the *Gazette*. No. Two or three hours with a yelping tabloid. I begin at the foot of the column and toil my way up the page to find each story unedifyingly summarized in inch-high type. MAN GIVES BIRTH TO DOG. Or STARLET RAPED BY PTERODACTYL. Greta Garbo, I read, has been reborn as a cat. All this stuff about *twins*. A Nordic superrace will shortly descend from the cosmic iceclouds; they will rule the earth for a thousand years. All this stuff about *Atlantis*. Appropriately, it is the garbage people who bring me my reading matter. I haul in the bags—which emanate, it would seem, from the monstrous jaws, the industrial violence, of the garbage truck. And so I sit here gurgling into my glass and soaking up all that moronic drek. I can't help it. I'm at Tod's mercy. What's going on—in the world, I mean? I wouldn't know about that either. Except when Tod's eye strays from the Kwik Crossword in the *Gazette*. Most of the time I'm staring fixedly at stuff like *Opposite of small (3)* or *Not dirty (5)*. There is a bookcase in the living room. Beyond its dusty glass, the dusty spines, all standing to attention. But no. Instead, LOVE LIFE ON PLUTO. I AM ZSA ZSA GABOR SAYS MONKEY. SIAMESE QUINS!

There are certain pluses now, though, as the years lurch past. The Reagan Era, I think, is doing wonders for Tod's morale.

Physically I'm in great shape. My ankles and knees and spine and neck no longer hurt all the time—or not all at once, anyway. I get to places much quicker than I used to: places like the far end of the room. I'm there before you know it. My bearing is almost princely. I sold that stick of mine long ago.

Tod and I are feeling so terrific that we've joined a club and taken up tennis. Perhaps prematurely. Because—to begin with, at least—it made our back ache like a son of a bitch. Tennis is a pretty dumb game, I'm finding: the fuzzy ball jumps out of the net, or out of the chicken wire at the back of the court, and the four of us bat it around until it is pocketed—quite arbitrarily, it seems to me—by the server. Yet we leap and snort away, happily enough. We josh and kid: our trusses, our elbow supports. *Pap* say the rackets. Tod is popular; the guys appear to like him fine. I don't know what Tod makes of them, except that his glands tell me he could do without any special attention, or any attention at all.

Most of the time we sit around the clubroom playing cards. The clubroom is where I see the President, on the mounted TV. Yes, the old guys, the elderly parties with their freckles and fruit juices, they all get a big kick out of the President: his frowns, his bloopers, his world-class hair. Tod likes it in the clubroom, but there is a man here whom he hates and fears. The man's name is Art—another gorilla of a granddad, with a murderous backslap and a voice of millennial penetration and power. Even I was terrified the first time it happened, when Art rolled over to our table, gave Tod a kind of rabbit punch that almost broke his neck, and said, incredibly loudly,

"You eat them alive."

"Yes. What?" said Tod.

He leaned closer. "Others in here might buy that shit, Friendly, but I know what you're after."

"Oh, that's been much exaggerated."

"Still chasing them?" Art shouted, and rolled away again.

Every time we try to slip past Art's table, there'll be a pause, and then a thick whisper that beats its way right

13

across the room: "Tod Friendly: had more ass than a toilet seat." Tod doesn't like that. He doesn't like that one bit.

Nevertheless, in the Superette, these days, it's true, the eyes of Tod Friendly linger on the bodies of the local frauleins as they tug their carts. The ankles, the join of the hips, the inlet of the clavicle, the hair. It turns out, too, that Tod has a black chest with photographs of women in it. Gay old broads in party dresses and tan pants suits. Ribboned letters, lockets, the knickknacks of love. Deeper down in the chest, where Tod doesn't often burrow, the women get appreciably younger and are to be seen in things like shorts and swimwear. If this all means what I think it means, then I'm impatient. I really can't wait. I don't know how much sense it makes to say that I am tiring of Tod's company. We are in this together, absolutely. But it isn't good for him to be so alone. *His* isolation is complete. Because he doesn't know I'm here.

We're picking up new habits all the time. Bad habits, I'm assuming: solitary, anyway. Tod sins singly. . . . He has acquired a taste for alcohol and tobacco. He starts the day with these vices—the quiet glass of red wine, the thoughtful cigar—and isn't that meant to be especially bad? The other thing is this. Not very enthusiastically, and not at all sucessfully either, so far as I can ascertain, we have begun doing a sexual thing with ourself. That happens, *when* it happens, the minute we wake up. Then we stagger to our feet and pick our clothes off the floor, and sit and drool into our glass, puffing on a pensive perfecto, and staring at the tabloid and all its gruesome crap.

I can't tell—and I need to know—whether Tod is kind. Or how unkind. He takes toys from children, on the street. He does. The kid will be standing there, with flustered mother,

14

with big dad. Tod'll come on up. The toy, the squeaky duck or whatever, will be offered to him by the smiling child. Tod takes it. And backs away, with what I believe is called a shit-eating grin. The child's face turns blank, or closes. Both toy and smile are gone: he takes both toy and smile. Then he heads for the store, to cash it in. For what? A couple of bucks. Can you believe this guy? He'll take candy from a baby, if there's fifty cents in it for him. Tod goes to church and everything. He trudges along there on a Sunday, in hat, tie, dark suit. The forgiving look you get from everybody on the way in—Tod seems to need it, the social reassurance. We sit in lines and worship a corpse. But it's clear what Tod's after. Christ, he's so shameless. He always takes a really big bill from the bowl.

It's all strange to me. I know I live on a fierce and magical planet, which sheds or surrenders rain or even flings it off in whipstroke after whipstroke, which fires out bolts of electric gold into the firmament at 186,000 miles per second, which with a single shrug of its tectonic plates can erect a city in half an hour. Creation . . . is easy, is quick. There's also a universe, apparently. But I cannot bear to see the stars, even though I know they're there all right, and I do see them, because Tod looks upward at night, as everybody does, and coos and points. The Plough. Sirius, the dog. The stars, to me, are like pins and needles, are like the routemap of a nightmare. Don't join the dots. . . . Of the stars, one alone can I contemplate without pain. And that's a planet. The planet they call the evening star, the morning star. Intense Venus.

There are love letters—I know it—in that black chest of Tod's. I tell myself to cultivate patience. Meanwhile, sometimes, I fold up and roughly seal and then dispatch letters I haven't written. Tod makes them, with fire. Over in the grate there. Later, we stroll out and pop them in our mailbox, which says T. T. FRIENDLY. They are letters to me, to us. For now, there's just this one correspondent. Some guy in New York. Always the same signature at the foot of the page. Always the same letter, come to that. It reads: "Dear Tod Friendly: I hope you are in good health. The weather here continues to be temperate! With best wishes. Yours sincerely . . ." These letters arrive annually, around the turn of the year. It wasn't long before I started finding them both repetitive and bland. Tod feels differently. For nights on end, before the letters come, his physiology speaks of alerted fear, of ignoble relief.

The moon I actually like looking at. Its face, at this time of the month, is especially craven and chinless, like the earth's exiled or demoted soul.

2

You have to be cruel to be kind

These developments all came one
after the other. A new home. A
career. The use of an automobile.

And a love life. What with all the activity and everything, I've hardly had a moment to myself.

The house move was a perfectly symmetrical operation: lucid, elegant. Big men came, and loaded all my stuff onto their pickup. I rode with them in the cab (we tossed the one-liners back and forth)—to our destination. Which was the city. Down Route 6, south of the river, over the tracks, beyond the stockyards and their rusty corsetry, their spinal supports, their arthritic suspenders. The new property is smaller than what we're used to: terraced, two up two down, with a modest backyard. I'm delighted with the place, because what I'm after, I suppose, is human variety, and America's pretty pluralism, and there's even more of that here. But Tod is in two minds about it. He's confused. I can tell. For instance, on the day we moved, while the men were still lurching around with their crates and cardboard boxes, Tod slipped out into the garden—the garden on which he had worked for so many years. He lowered himself to his knees, and, sniffing hungrily, richly . . . It was beautiful, in its way. Dewlike drops of moisture formed on the dry grass, and rose upward through the air as if powered by the jolts in our chest. The moisture bathed our cheeks, deliciously, until with our tickling eyes we drew it in. Such distress. Why? I assumed at the time that he was crying for the garden and what he'd done to it. The garden was heaven when we started out, but over the years, well, don't blame me is all I'm saying. It wasn't my decision. It never is. So Tod's tears were tears of remorse, or propitiation. For what he'd done. Look at it. A nightmare of wilt and mildew, of fungus and black spot. All the tulips and roses he patiently drained and crushed, then sealed their exhumed corpses and took them in the paper bag to the store for money. All the weeds and nettles he screwed into the soil—and the earth

18

took this ugliness, snatched at it with a sudden grip. Such, then, are the fruits of Tod's meticulous vandalism. Greenfly, whitefly, sawfly are his familiars. And horsefly. He seems to summon them to his face with a slow flick of the wrist. The muscle-bound horseflies retreat and return; they rest, rubbing their hands together in anticipation and spite. Destruction—is difficult. Destruction is slow.

Creation, as I said, is no trouble at all. Like with the car. One of the first things we do, after settling in—we show up at this little garage or car cemetery a few blocks south. I'd call this place a hole-in-the-wall operation. But there's no wall to hack a hole in. The buildings around here are right down on their knees. That's evidently the thing with the contemporary city. You might want to work in it. But no one is seriously expected to live in it. Content, meaning and content, are all stored uptown, in the notched pillars of the skyscrapers. Well, the car seemed okay. It seemed like any other car. But Tod looked at it with real feeling, with the dull heat of—I don't know—thwarted love. The garage guy soon joined him, wiping an oily rag with his oily fingers. Next, Tod goes and gives him eight hundred bucks. The man counts the money and they argue for a while, Tod saying nine hundred, the man saying seven, then the man saying six while Tod holds out for a thou, and so on. Left alone with the car, Tod ran his fingers along the bodywork. Searching for what? Scar tissue. Trauma . . . Tod was blue that morning anyway, as I recall. In the afternoon he'd attended a funeral, or just accidentally witnessed one, hanging back, rather, in the mournerless churchyard, where the graves were flush with the earth. He crossed himself and slipped away quickly. We rode the bus back, and buses take forever and are full of drunks and screaming children. . . . Cars are the thing. *Cars*. Every day we went back to the garage; and every day that car of ours was in sorrier shape. Eight hundred dollars? And you could actually see them at it, the grease monkeys, with hammers and spanners, about their long chore of patient wreckage.

Needless to say, by the time we went along to claim it (elsewhere: uptown), Tod's car was a regular bedpan. We weren't in top form either. The transaction included a most unwelcome preliminary. Hospital. That's right. A look-in at Casualty. We made our own way there (somehow Tod knows this town backward) and we didn't stay long, thank God. You do what you have to do: you take your shirt off and get prodded and tapped, but you keep your head down; you don't want to know about the stuff they do in there. It's not your place to speak out. It's none of your business. The paramedics eventually drove me uptown to the scene of the accident. There was my car, like a mad old hog caught in midspasm, its snout and tusks crushed and steaming. And I didn't feel too good myself as the police officer helped wedge me into its driving seat and tried to shut the warped front door. Thereafter I sat back and let Tod handle everything. There were all kinds of people staring in at us, and for a while Tod just stared stupidly back at them. But then he got on with it. He rammed his foot down on the brake and sent the car into a fizzing convulsion of rev and whinny. With a skillful lurch he gave the bent hydrant on the sidewalk a crunchy shouldercheck—and we were off, weaving at speed back up the street. Other cars screamed in to fill the sudden vacuum of our wake.

Minutes later: the first installment of our love life. Which was quite a coincidence. We came home, Tod flooring the accelerator to bring about a violent halt. He didn't pause to admire the car (the car seemed like new: great!) but hurried inside, flinging off his coat with a hot gasp and making a lunge for the phone.

I tried to concentrate. I think I got most of it. It went like this.

"Goodbye, Tod."

"Wait. Don't do anything."

"Who cares? It's all shit anyway."

"Irene," he said.

"Yes I am. Tod, I'm just this terrible old lady now. How'd it happen?"

"No you're not."

"No I'm not. I'm going to kill myself."

"No you're not."

"I'm going to call the *New York Times.*"

"Irene," he said, with a new heat in his voice. And a new heat all over his body.

"I know you changed your name. How about that! I know you ran."

"You know nothing."

"I'm going to tell on you."

"Oh yes?"

"You say it in the night. In your sleep."

"Irene."

"I know your secret."

"What is it?"

"I want you to know something."

"Irene, you're drunk."

"Piece of shit."

"Yes?" said Tod boredly—and hung up on her. He put the phone down and listened to its ringing—its machine persistence. And then its silence. His feeling tone was blank, was clear. . . . Well, after that, I suppose, things can only improve. I wished Tod would go and dig out that black chest of his, so that I could get a proper look at this Irene. But he didn't, of course. Fine chance.

* * *

21

Maybe love will be like driving.

"Pop? Your driving days are over." So said the mechanic in his oily dungarees. So said the hospital orderly in his stark white smock. But they were wrong. On the contrary, our driving days have just begun. I think Tod must be hankering for the old house, over to Wellport, because that's where most of our trips end up. He's kept a key. We go in and move from room to room. It's all empty now. He measures things. It's done with love, this measuring. More recently we've started inspecting other properties in the Wellport area. But none of them is worth measuring, like our old place. Back down Route 6 he slowly rolls.

We've started finding love letters, in the trash, letters from Irene. He looks them over with his head at an angle and stuffs them in a drawer somewhere. Maybe love will be like driving. When people move—when they travel—they look where they've come from, not where they're going. Is this what the human beings always do? Then love will be like driving, which doesn't appear to make much immediate sense. For example, you have five reverse gears and only one for forward, which is marked R, for Reverse. When we drive, we don't look where we're going. We look where we came from. There are accidents, sure, and yet it all works out. The city streams and pours in this symphony of trust.

My career . . . I don't want to talk about it. You don't want to hear about it. One night I got out of bed and drove—very badly—to an office. I then had a party with all my new colleagues. At six o'clock I went to the room with my name on the desk, donned a white coat, and started work. What at? Doctoring!

As life speeds up like this I move among the urban people, in the urban setting, the city's metal and mortar, its sharper

interactions, with more grit and bite in the gears. The city—
and there are bigger cities than this (like New York, where
the weather, I learn, continues to be temperate)—the city
does things to the people who live in it. Does most things,
perhaps, to the people who shouldn't *be* in the city. Not
now. They are the wrong people in the wrong place at the
wrong time. Irene shouldn't be in the city. Tod's at home
here, in some ways. He has stopped driving out to Wellport
but I bet he misses our time there, its vigorlessness so safe
and morally neutral, when he wore the passive uniform of
old age. The old aren't cruel, are they. We don't look to the
old, to the stooped, for cruelty. Cruelty, which is bright-
eyed, which is pink-tongued . . .

This is more than city. This is inner city. And despite
his newfound professional status, Tod lives among the
underclass. Under, inner—how do these conditions express
themselves? Jesus, how do cities get here? One can just about
imagine the monstrous labors of the eventual demolition
(centuries away, long after my time), and the eventual creation of the pleasant land—the green, the promised. But I'm
awfully glad I wasn't around for the city's arrival. It must
have just lurched into life. It must have just lurched into life
out of a great trodden stillness of dust and damp. My colleagues at work, they tend to reside, prudently and intelligibly enough, up on the Hill or in the eastern suburbs, toward
the ocean. But perhaps Tod Friendly has need of the city,
where he can always drift among others, where he is never
considered singly.

My career move? One night about a month ago Tod
woke up in an unusually desperate condition, half clothed,
in fact, and with everything intolerably slewing around
him—as if the bedroom was moored to a loosening capstan
inside his gut, where his secret moans. I thought: No wonder

I felt so terrible yesterday. For yesterdays are always terrible, when Tod hits the tea. Then he upped and did something . . . "significant": coyly significant. We went into the living room and seized the brass clock that has always adorned the shelf above our fireplace (oh, what strong hands he has), and violently enclosed it in the festive wrapping paper he found in the trash. Tod stood there for a moment, staring at the clock's face, and then the mirror's face, with a sallow smile. The room was still circling around us. Counterclockwise. In the car we bounded off to the reception at AMS, or Associated Medical Services, on Route 6. Tod, incidentally, unloaded our clock on one of the nurses, little Maureen. Little Maureen was agitated, but she made a nice speech. Little Maureen, whose face so disturbed me, fair, freckled, abjectly Nordic, the mouth too big or just too external, designed to express only powerlessness. Powerlessness: hope and no-hope, both at the same time.

Well I can't pretend that this doctoring business came as a total surprise. For a while now the narrow house has been filling up with medical paraphernalia, with doctoring tackle. Books about anatomy, born from fire in the backyard. Prescription pads. A plastic skull. One day Tod took from the trash a framed certificate and went and hung it on the toilet doornail. With amusement he surveyed the wrought script—for several minutes. And of course I get a big boost when something like this happens, because words make plain sense, even though Tod always reads them backward.

I swear by Apollo Physician, by Health, by Panacea, and by all the gods and goddesses, making them my witnesses, that I will carry out, according to my ability and judgment, this oath and this indenture. . . . I will keep pure and holy both my life and my art. In whatsoever houses I enter, I will enter to help the sick, and I will abstain from all intentional wrongdoing and harm. . . .

Tod had a good laugh at that. . . . Also, the characteristic black bag, swung out of a closet. Inside, a world of pain.

A little stadium of pain, with darkness at the bottom of it.

Irene telephones Tod regularly now. I suppose it's good that we should get to know each other: first. She is calm and (usually) sober; Tod accepts these calls as one of his many duties, and settles down to them with resignation, with whiskey glass, with patient perfecto. Irene says she is sad. She is lonely. She finds she is less and less inclined to blame Tod for her unhappiness. She says she knows he's a bastard and can't understand why she loves him. . . . Nor can I. But love is strange. Love is strange. Sometimes she contemplates—quite dispassionately, it must be admitted—the option of suicide. Tod warns her that such talk is sinful. Personally, I think we can dismiss *suicide* as a hollow threat. I've been thinking about it. Suicide *isn't* an option, is it. Not in this world. Once you're here, once you're on board, you can't get off. You can't get out.

She weeps, controllably. Tod keeps his counsel. She's sorry. He's sorry. That's the way it is.

I hope he makes it up to her in the end.

The actual doctoring I've become pretty stoical about. Not that I have any say in the matter. I don't give the orders around here. I don't wear the pants. So stoicism, I reckon, is my only hope. Tod and I seem to be on top of the work, and nobody has complained so far. So far, too, we've been spared any of the gorier stuff they do here—and some of this stuff you just wouldn't believe. Surprisingly, Tod is

known and mocked and otherwise celebrated for his squea-
mishness. I say surprisingly because I happen to know Tod
isn't squeamish. *I'm* squeamish. I'm the squeamish one. Oh,
Tod can hack it. His feeling tone—aweless, distant—is quite
secure against the daily round in here, the stares of vigil,
the smell of altered human flesh. Tod can take all this—
whereas I'm harrowed by it. From my point of view, work
is an eight-hour panic attack. You can imagine me curled up
within, feebly gagging, and trying to avert my eyes. . . . I'm
taking on the question of violence, this most difficult question. Intellectually I can just about accept that violence is
salutary, that violence is good. But I can find nothing in me
that assents to its ugliness. I was always this way, I realize,
even back in Wellport. A child's breathless wailing calmed
by the firm slap of the father's hand, a dead ant revived by
the careless press of a passing sole, a wounded finger healed
and sealed by the knife's blade: anything like that made me
flinch and veer. But the body I live and move in, Tod's
body, feels nothing.

We seem to specialize in the following areas: paperwork,
gerontology, maladies of the central nervous system, and
what they call *talkdown*. I sit there in my white coat, with
my reflex hammer, tuning forks, small flashlight, tongue
blades, pins, needles. My patients are even older than I am.
It has to be said that they usually look fairly cheerful on
their way in. They turn, and sit, and nod bravely. "Good,"
says Tod. The old party then says, "Thank you, Doctor,"
and hands over his prescription. Tod takes the scrap of paper
and does his little stunt with the pen and pad.

"I'm going to let you have something," Tod says
grandly, "that will make you feel better." Which is the pur-
est bull, I know: any second now—so invasively, so grimly,
and on the basis of so little acquaintance—Tod's going to
stick his finger up the poor guy's ass.

"More scared," says the patient, unbuckling his belt.

"You seem fine to me," says Tod. "For your age. Do you feel depressed?"

After the business on the couch (a rotten deal for both of us: how we all whimper), Tod'll do stuff like palpate the carotid arteries in the neck and the temporal arteries just in front of the ears. Then the wrists. Then the bell of the stethoscope is deployed, low on the forehead, just above the orbits. "Close your eyes," says Tod to the patient, who, of course, immediately opens them. "Take my hand. Raise your left arm. Good. Just relax for a while." Then it's *talk-down*, which will typically go like this:

Tod: "It might start a panic."

Patient: "Shout *fire*."

Tod: "What would you do if you were in a theater and you saw flames and smoke?"

Patient: "Sir?"

Tod pauses. "That's an abnormal response. The normal response would be: 'Nobody's perfect, so don't criticize others.' "

"They'll break the glass," says the patient, frowning.

"What is meant by the saying 'People in glass houses shouldn't throw stones?' "

"Uh, seventy-six. Eighty-six."

"What's ninety-three minus seven?"

"1914–1918."

"What are the dates of the First World War?"

"Okay," says the patient, sitting up straight.

"I'm now going to ask you some questions."

"No."

"Sleeping okay? Any digestive problems?"

"I'll be eighty-one in January."

"And you're . . . what?"

"I don't feel myself."

"Well, what seems to be the problem?"

And that's it. They certainly don't look too cheerful on their way out. They back off from me with their eyes wide. And they're gone. Pausing only to do that creepy thing— knocking, quietly, on your door. At least I can say that I do these old guys no real or lasting harm. Unlike nearly all the other patients at AMS, they go out of here in no worse shape than when they came in.

The social standing enjoyed by doctors is of course formidably high. When you move, as a doctor, through society, with your white coat, your black bag, the eyes of others seek you upward. Mothers express it best: their postures seem to concede that you have the power over their children; as a doctor, you can leave the children alone, and you can take them away, and you can bring them back, if you choose to. Yes, we walk tall. Us doctors. Our presence chastens others, renders other serious. The tilted eyes of the others gives the doctor his heroic, questing mein, his humorless nimbus. The biological soldier. And for what? . . . One thing that's helping me through it, aside from my chats with Irene, is that Tod and I are feeling so damn good these days: physically. I can't understand why Tod doesn't show more gratitude for the improvement. When I think back to how things were out in Wellport, man, we were still walking, but only just. It was taking us twenty-five minutes to cross the room. We can bend over now with scarcely a groan, scarcely a knee-crackle. We're up and down those stairs—hey, where's the fire? Occasionally we get spare bits of our body back, from the trash. A tooth, a nail. Extra hair. The effortful shepherding of one's confusion and faint nausea, which I assumed was the basic existential package, turns out to have been a temporary condition. And sometimes, and sometimes for minutes on end (especially if you're lying down), nothing hurts.

Tod doesn't appreciate the improvement. Well, if he does, he's pretty nonchalant about it. On the whole. But get this. You know that sexual thing we started doing, so very perfunctorily, out in Wellport, that sexual thing with ourself? Tod's working at it much harder now. In celebration, perhaps, of his increasing vigor—or as a form of training. All the same, it's by no means clear to me that we're making any progress. . . . Tod? I don't know. How is it for you? Any good? Because from my point of view it's still a total flop.

His dreams are full of figures who scatter in the wind like leaves, full of souls who form constellations like the stars I hate to see. Tod is conducting a long argument, and he is telling the truth, but the invisible people who might hear and judge luckily refuse to believe him and turn away in silence, weariness, and disgust. Often he is resignedly mutilated by sour aldermen, by painfully fat lord mayors, by put-upon railway porters. Sometimes he glows with great power, which rushes out and solves and clears everything: a power lent by the tutelary maker who presides over all his sleep.

The pimps, and the little hookers . . .

I puzzle at the local economy, the commerce, the apologetic arrangements of the ignored, of the cooled city. And this I get plenty of opportunity to do—to puzzle at it, I mean. I puzzle a lot, if the truth be known. In fact I've had to conclude that I am generally rather slow on the uptake. Possibly even subnormal, or mildly autistic. It may very well be that I'm not playing with a full deck. The cards won't add up for me; the world won't start making sense. It's certainly the case that I appear to be hitched up with Tod like this, but he's not to know I'm here. And I'm lonely. . . . Tod Friendly, stocky, emollient Tod Friendly, moves around at large in the city's substructures, the shelters, the centers, the halfway houses, the flops. He isn't one of the entrenched busybodies or Little Annie Fixits who, for pressing personal reasons, somehow need to police these mysterious institutions, where *abuse* is the buzzword. He comes and goes. He suggests and directs and recommends. He's one of grief's middlemen. For life here is junkie, is hooker, is single-parent, is no fixed abode.

Hookers have this thing for mature men. They do. You hardly ever see them bothering with guys their own age. Watchfully the johns back their way into the significant rooms, the short-lease apartments of the low tenement on Herrera, a building that basks in its own brand of damp and dread. An act of love occurs, for which the john, or the *trick* as he's called, for some reason, will be swiftly remunerated. Afterward the fond couple will stroll back onto the street, and part. The men slope off, looking ashamed of themselves (doing it for money like that). But the hooker will ravenously remain, on the sidewalk, in tank top, in hotpants, killing time before her next date. Or hitching rides to nowhere with the additional old stiffs who cruise by in their cunning old cars. Tod is quite often to be found in the tenement of whores. He's a senior citizen, so the girls are forever putting their moves on him. But Tod's not there for the sex and the dough. On the contrary. *He* shells out (token sums, like a couple of bucks), and invariably keeps his pants on (he doesn't even consider them; they are other). Basically it seems that Tod scores drugs here. Not for his personal use: the tetracycline, the methadone—it all finds its way back to the pharmacy at AMS. Then, too, there are physical injuries to be tackled, in the tenement on Herrera, with its twisted sheets, its stained bidets.

At the flops, the bums all eat the same thing. Unlike in a restaurant or the AMS commissary. It isn't good, I think, when everyone eats the same thing. I know that none of us has any choice about what we eat; it's all down to drainage, and some systems are obviously better than others. But I get a woozy feeling when I watch them spoon away, and the plates—twenty or thirty of them—all fill up with the same thing. . . . The women at the crisis centers and the refuges are all hiding from their redeemers. The crisis center is not called a crisis center for nothing. If you want a crisis, just check in. The welts, the abrasions and the black eyes get starker, more livid, until it is time for the women to return, in an ecstasy of distress, to the men who will suddenly heal them. Some require more specialized treatment. They stagger off and go and lie in a park or a basement or wherever, until men come along and rape them, and then they're okay again. Ah shit, says Brad, the repulsive orderly, there's nothing wrong with them—meaning the women in the shelter— that a good six inches won't cure. Tod frowns at him sharply. I hate Brad too, and I hate to say it, but sometimes he's absolutely right. How could the world fix it so that someone like Brad could ever be right?

I don't see eye to eye with Tod on all issues. Far from it. For instance, Tod's very down on the pimps. The pimps—these outstanding individuals, who, moreover, lend such color to the city scene, with their zootily customized clothes and cars. Where would the poor girls be without their pimps, who shower money on them and ask for nothing in return? Not like Tod and his tender mercies. He just goes around there to rub dirt in their wounds. And backs off quick, before the longsuffering pimp shows up, and knocks the girl into shape with his jeweled fists. As he works, the baby in the cot beside the bed will hush its weeping, and sleep angelically, secure in the knowledge that the pimp is come.

*   *   *

31

Irene still telephones regularly but I mustn't get my hopes up. I thought she was slowly coming round to us. She isn't. She's turned against us again, with a vengeance. Why, I don't know. Is it something we've said?

It's mildly encouraging now, though, when Tod looks at a woman in the street. For once his eyes point where I want them to point. Our imperatives or priorities are by no means entirely congruent, but at least they overlap. We like the same kind of woman—the womanly kind. Tod looks first at the face; then the breasts; then the lower abdomen. If it's a back view, he goes: hair; waist; rump. Neither of us, it would seem, is much of a leg man, but I suppose I could do with a bit more than I get. I'm also annoyed by the timespots Tod allows for each section. He is done with the face way too soon. A single downward swipe of the eyes. Whereas I'd like to linger. Maybe the etiquette forbids this. Still, I'm mildly encouraged. There's hardly any of the usual vertigo effect, when I'm trying to see things he's not looking at, when I'm trying to look at things he's not seeing.

Vivified, perhaps, by all this fieldwork we're doing, our lone sex sessions have, of late, become unrecognizably livelier. The missing component, the extra essence, is to be found, of course, in the toilet. Or in the trash.

Where would Tod and I be without the toilet? Where would we be without all the trash?

Mothers bring Tod their babies in the night. Tod discourages this—but he's usually pretty sympathetic. The mothers pay him in antibiotics, which often seem to be the cause of the babies' pain. You have to be cruel to be kind. The babies are no better when they leave, patiently raising hell all the way to the door. And the moms crack up completely: they go out of here *wailing*. It's understandable. I understand. I know how people disappear. Where do they disappear to? Don't ask that question. Never ask it. It's none of your business. The little children on the street, they get littler and littler. At some point it is thought necessary to confine them to strollers, later to backpacks. Or they are held in the arms and quietly soothed—of course they're sad to be going. In the very last months they cry more than ever. And no longer smile. The mothers then proceed to the hospital. Where else? Two people go into that room, that room with the forceps, the soiled bib. Two go in. But only one comes out. Oh, the poor mothers, you can see how they feel during the long goodbye, the long goodbye to babies.

And about time too.

Now that it's eventually started happening, I find that my attitude is one of high indignation. Why has Tod been frittering my life away like this? Overnight the world has opened up and revealed its depth and color. And the self has opened up, also. We're not just surface anymore but voluminous and deep-sea, with our wiggling flora, our warped fish. Everybody's like this, I realize: touchingly—no, grippingly—vulnerable. We have nowhere to hide.

Love didn't catch me entirely unawares—I had fair warning. Love was heralded by a whole new bunch of love letters. But these weren't love letters from Irene. They were love letters *to* Irene. Written by Tod. In his squat and unvarying hand. They came from the trash, of course, from the innards of a ten-gallon Hefty. Tod went and sat in the living room with this red-ribboned bundle on his lap. He had his black chest out too. Then after a pause he took a letter at random from the middle of the stack; he stared at it with an unfocused, an uncommitted eye. I made out what I could:

33

My dear Irene,

> *Thank you again for the cushions. I do like them. They brighten up the room as well as making it more "cozy" . . . quite ruined. With scrambled eggs it is better to leave the pot standing with cold water, not hot . . . You must not get too concerned about this matter of your veins, which are superficial. There is no pigmentation and no edema. Remember I like you just the way you are . . . I look forward to seeing you on Tuesday with the usual impatience but Friday might be more convenient. . . .*

Blankly Tod turned to that chest of his. The photograph he wanted was all crushed and curled but he soon healed it with a squeeze of his fist. . . . Wow, I thought. So she's the one. No spring chicken. And a really *big* old broad. Smiling, in a tan pants suit. When he went to work that evening, Tod left the letters by the front step, encased in a white shoebox on which someone—presumably Irene—had scrawled the words *The Hell with You*. It didn't seem like a very good sign. But then Tod's letter, in my view, wasn't very promising either.

Two nights later he woke up in the small hours and lay there coldly. "Shtib," he grunted. Tod's been doing this quite a bit lately—grunting: Shtib. Shtib. I thought it might be a cough, or a half-stoppered eructation, or just some unalluring new vagary. Then I caught on to what it was the guy was saying. He climbed out of bed and opened the window. And it began. In waves, in subtle gusts, the room began to fill with the warmth and spoor of another being. Most noticeably, and surprisingly, cigarette smoke!—which Tod has a big thing about, for all his periodic perfectos. Something pastelike and candyish, too, something sweet and old.

These were the smells she was sending across the city. . . . Unhurriedly Tod slipped out of his pajamas and donned his fibrous dressing gown. He then discomposed the bedding with an inconvenienced air. Still, he prepared her cigarettes for her at least, filling a saucer with a few butts and plenty of ash. We closed the window and went downstairs and waited.

It showed good form—and was, I ventured to imagine, rather romantic of Tod—to go outside like that and stand in his slippers on the wet sidewalk. Though his mood at this stage, I admit, seemed, if anything, to be one of exhaustive disenchantment. Very soon we heard her car, its slithery approach, and saw the twin red lights at the end of the street. She parked, and opened the car door loudly, and squeezed out. I was slightly taken aback when she walked *forward* across the road, shaking her head in sorrow or denial. A really big old broad. Irene. That's right.

"Tod?" she said. "This is it. Happy now?"

Happy or not, Tod preceded her through the front door. She wrenched off her coat while Tod trudged on up, and she came pounding after him. I was discouraged, I confess. I was hurt. Because this was my first time. Call me a fool, call me a dreamer—I was hoping it would all be beautiful. But no. I have to go and catch her on a really bad day. She wasn't what she wanted to be either. Oh, can't we work this out? Tod and I reclined on the wrung bedding as Irene advanced into the room, holding a tightly gripped paper tissue to her eyes and calling us a piece of shit.

Then she started taking her clothes off. Women!

"Irene," Tod reasoned. "Irene. Irene."

She undressed quickly, as if against time; but the speed of her movements had nothing to do with desire. She talked quickly too, and wept, and shook her head. A big old broad, in big white sweater, big white pants. Her breasts formed a bluff beneath her chin, sharply triangular and aerodynamic, and kept aloft, ultimately, by some kind of G.I. Joe backpack of hawsers and winches. Off came the carapace of her corset. Then that big white tush was ambling toward me. And I thought her *clothes* were white. What was she saying, Irene, what was she going on about, in words half-saved, half-drowned—in gasps and whispers? In summary, this: that men were either too dull or too pointed with nothing in between. Too dumb or too smart. Too innocent, too guilty.

"Bad joke," said Tod as she turned and looked down on us. "You know I didn't mean that."

Irene *seemed* to relent. Her shape descended and she settled herself beside me, in awkward abundance, and my hand reached out to the white pulp of her shoulder. Astounding proximity. Never, never before . . . She was tense and tight (as I was); but skin is soft. Touch it. It gives. It gives to the touch.

"Great," said Tod. "Then you can get the hell out of here."

These words, I'm glad to say, had a relaxing effect on her. But her voice still sounded frightened when she said, "I promise."

"You promise?"

"Never," she said.

"You wouldn't?"

"But I'd never tell."

"Oh what nonsense," said Tod. "Who would believe you anyway? You just don't know enough."

"Sometimes I think that's the only reason you go on with this. You're scared I'm going to tell."

There was a silence. Irene moved even closer as the conversation took another turn.

"Life," said Tod.

"What?" said Irene.

"Christ, who cares. It's all shit anyway."

"Why? I just don't rate, huh?"

"That's something you don't ever talk about."

"Were you this nice to your wife and kid?"

"We wouldn't know about that, would we, Irene."

"Except to your friends. And family. Your loved ones."

"You have no obligation to be healthy."

"Also fatal," said Irene.

"Do you really have to do that? It's a disgusting habit."

Tod started coughing and flapping his thick right hand about. After a while Irene quenched her cigarette of its fire and restored it to the pack. She turned toward us meaningfully. There followed about ten minutes of what I guess you'd call foreplay. Snuggling, grunting, sighing—that kind of thing. Then he moved, and loomed above her. And as she opened her legs I was flooded by thoughts and feelings I'd never had before. To do with power.

"Oh baby," she said, and kissed my cheek. "It doesn't matter."

"I'm sorry," said Tod. "I'm so sorry."

Well, they made it up, anyway. Afterward, it was very much easier. Yes, the atmosphere was outstanding as we put our clothes on and went downstairs to have something to eat. There we sat, at the dinette feature, side by side, equably untwirling yard after yard of the pale pasta. Then—another first—off to the movies, if you please. And arm in arm. I felt I was moving through a strange land, on tiptoe, with the woman I was allowed to touch—was allowed to do anything I wanted to, or at least anything I was capable of doing. What's the limit? As we walked a siren sounded, like a wolf-whistle caught on a scratched record. . . . The movie

37

passed off fine also. I was worried at first, when Irene started crying again before we had even taken our seats. And I suppose the film was pretty depressing. All about love. The on-screen couple, quietly glowing with beauty and amusement—they seemed made for each other; but after various misunderstandings and adventures they ended up going their separate ways. By this time Irene was emitting a steady gurgle of contentment, when she wasn't laughing her head off. Everyone was laughing. But not Tod. Not Tod. To be fair, I didn't think it was funny either. We ended up at a bar near the theater. She had stingers. Tod with his steins. And although Tod walked home in a filthy temper (he was thoroughly out of sorts), our parting with Irene was marked by its cordiality and warmth. I know I'm going to be seeing a lot more of her. On top of which we came out twenty-eight dollars to the good. Make that thirty-one with the popcorn. It doesn't sound like much but you've got to watch out these days, with everything constantly getting cheaper and Tod grimly counting his money the whole time.

Me, I'm head over heels. I don't know whether I'm coming or going. The forgiveness offered by her young blue eyes, which peep out in mortal embarrassment from the old sneaker of her face, so puffed, so pinched, so parched. Mmm—people! It seems to me that you need a lot of courage, or a lot of something, to enter into others, into other people. We all think that everyone else lives in fortresses, in fastnesses: behind moats, behind sheer walls studded with spikes and broken glass. But in fact we inhabit much punier structures. We are, it turns out, all jerry-built. Or not even. You can just stick your head under the flap of the tent and crawl right in. If you get the okay.

So perhaps escape is possible. Escape from the—from the indecipherable monad. As for her journey into him, well, that's tougher. She tells us things about ourself. But how much does she really know? Tod's playing it cool, of course, as always. I still don't know if he'll ever come across.

It's quite exciting, I suppose—the news about my wife and child. The wife and child that Tod and I will one day have. But babies worry me. We do know, naturally, that babies are always causing worry and concern. They are very worrying little creatures.

Where do they go, the little creatures who disappear: the vanished? I have an intractable presentiment that I will soon start seeing them in Tod's dream.

Every sixth or seventh day or so, in the morning, as we prepare to sack out, and go through the stunned routines of miring, of mussing (we derange each eyebrow with a fingerstroke against the grain), Tod and I can feel the dream just waiting to happen, gathering its energies from somewhere on the other side. We're fatalistic. We lie there, with the lamp burning, while dawn fades. Tepid sweats form, and shine, and instantly evaporate. Then our heart rate climbs, steadily, until our ears are gulping on the new blood. Now we don't know who we are. I have to be ready for when Tod makes his lunge for the light switch. And then in darkness with a shout that gives a fierce twist to his jaw—we're in it. The enormous figure in the white coat, his black boots straddling many acres. Somewhere down there, between his legs, the line of souls. I wish I had power, just power enough to avert my eyes. Please, don't show me the babies. . . . Where does the dream come from? He hasn't done it yet. So the dream must be about what Tod will eventually do.

There is a thing out there called *fashion*. Fashion is for youth and all its volatility, but Tod and I occasionally dabble. For example, we went to the thrift store not so long ago and picked up two pairs of flared pants. I wanted to try them on right there but for months he let them dangle in the closet upstairs, growing the wrinkles and air pockets that would finally fit his shape, the peculiar wishbone of his shanks. Then, one night, he unceremoniously slipped into them. Later, after work, I got a pretty good look at these new pants of ours, as Tod stood before the full-length mirror unknotting the plump Windsor of his tie. Well, they weren't actually outrageous, Tod's flares, nothing like the twin-ball-gown effect we would soon start seeing on the street. But I found them thoroughly disgraceful, all the same: aesthetically, they worked on me like violence. This substantial citizen, this old doctor—and his slobbering calves. Where have his *feet* gone, for Christ's sake? I knew then, I think, that Tod's cruelty, his secret, had to do with a central mistake about human bodies. Or maybe I just discovered something to do with the style or the *line* of his cruelty. Tod's cruelty would be trashy, shitty, errant, bassackward: flared. . . . Still, the pants caught on and now everyone is into them. They move down the street like yachts: the landlocked sailors of the city. Next thing you know, women's hemlines go up by about three feet. The sudden candor and power of female haunch. They're already coming down again, slowly, but Jesus.

Probably human cruelty is fixed and eternal. Only styles change. A few years ago, the pedophile, strolling through the shopping mall, or sitting at a quiet table in Salad Binge or Just Desserts, might have coordinated his assignations—his intergenerational trysts—by mobile telephone. Now you never see mobile telephones, and malls and restaurants are different, so the pedophile must manage things in some other way, in some other style.

A war is coming. Just a little one, for now. Several

times, in bars, glancing up from our Bud or our Molson or our Miller, we have seen that same shot on the mounted TV: like a eugenic cross between swordfish and stingray, the helicopter twirls upward from the ocean and crouches grimly on the deck of the aircraft carrier, ready to fight.

You'd think it might be quite relaxing, having (effectively) no will, and no body anyway through which to exercise it. Many administrative and executive matters, it's true, are taken right out of your hands. Yet there is always the countervailing desire to put yourself forward, to take your stand as the valuable exception. Don't just go along. Never just go along. Small may not be beautiful. But big is crazy.

I don't want to sound too flame-eyed and low-blink-rate about it—and, all right, I know I'm a real simp in many areas—but I'd say I was way ahead of Tod on this basic question of human *difference*. Tod has a sensing mechanism that guides his responses to all identifiable subspecies. His feeling tone jolts into specialized attitudes and readinesses: one for Hispanics, one for Asians, one for Arabs, one for Amerindians, one for blacks, one for Jews. And he has a secondary repertoire of alerted hostility toward pimps, hookers, junkies, the insane, the clubfooted, the hairlipped, the homosexual male, and the very old. (Here, incidentally, is my take on the homosexual male. It may be relevant. The homosexual male is fine—is pretty good news, in fact, on the whole—*so long as he knows he's homosexual*. It's when he is, and thinks he isn't: then there's confusion. Then there's danger. The way Tod feels about men, about women, about children: there is confusion. There is danger. Don't get me wrong. I'm not fingering Tod for a fruit, not exactly. I'm just saying that things might be less confused, and less dangerous, if he could soberly entertain the idea of being homosexual. That's what I'm saying.)

All these distinctions I've had to learn up on. Originally at least I had no preselected feelings about anybody, one way or the other (except about doctors: now where did *that* come from?). When I meet people, I wait for a pulse from their inner being, which tells me things like—how much fear, how much hate, how much peace, how much forgiveness. I suppose I really am the soulful type. Visualize the body I don't have, and see this: a sentimentalized fetus, with faithful smile.

There's a graduate student at AMS who's Japanese, over from Osaka on a six-month exchange deal, companionable enough at first, of course, but becoming increasingly glazed and remote. He's lucky he wasn't here a few years ago, when we really *hated* the Japanese. His name is Mikio, funny-looking kid, with his heavy cargo of otherness: his light-holding hair, his coated eyeballs and their meniscus of severe understanding. During his lunch break, in the AMS commissary, Mikio will sit buckled over a book. I've watched him, from a distance. He reads the way I read—or would read, if I ever got the chance. He turns the pages from right to left. He begins at the beginning and ends at the end. This makes a quirky sense to me—but Mikio and I are definitely in the minority here. And how can we two be right? It would make so many others wrong. Water moves upward. It seeks the highest level. What did you expect? Smoke falls. Things are created in the violence of fire. But that's all right. Gravity still pins us to the planet.

Many coworkers—Tod included—razz him about it and everything, but Mikio is free to do this, to read in his own way. Observant Jews, I've noticed, read this way too. People are free, then, they are generally free, then, are they? Well they don't *look* free. Tipping, staggering, with croaked or choking voices, blundering backward along lines seemingly already crossed, already mapped. Oh, the disgusted look on women's faces as they step backward through a doorway, out of the rain. Never watching where they are going, the people move through something prearranged, armed with lies. They're always looking forward to going places they've just come back from, or regretting doing things they haven't yet done. They say hello when they mean goodbye. Lords of lies and trash—all kings of crap and trash. Signs say No Littering—but who to? We wouldn't dream of it. Government does that, at night, with trucks; or uniformed men come sadly at morning with their trolleys, dispensing our rubbish, and shit for the dogs.

I mustn't become a bore on the subject, but I have to say that in physical terms Tod and I are now feeling absolutely terrific. Corporeal life is not without its minor indignities. We still take it in the ass every morning, along with everybody else—but the whole thing's over in a trice these days. Tod, I salute you: what bowl know-how, what can can-do. I was more or less resigned to a lifetime of the tearful half hour. But now we're out of there after a tearful twenty minutes.

Each day, before the mirror, as I inspect Tod's humanity—he shows no sign of noticing the improvement. It's almost as if he has no point of comparison. I want to click my heels, I want to clench my fist: *Yes*. Why aren't people happier about how great they're feeling, relatively? Why don't we hug each other all the time, saying, "How *about* this?"

Accordingly, after many false starts, after many hours in the sunless sea of bafflement, apology, and flopsweat, Tod and I have finally cut it with Irene. She was impeccably tactful, and drew no extra attention to the breakthrough.

43

Tod also played it cool: all in a day's work. But I was ecstatic. I was beside myself with pride. Almost certainly I was overreacting, as usual. I've calmed down a little. Now I'm just gorgeously smug. This is love. This is life. The knack, the trick: there turns out to be nothing to it. Life and love go together. It comes natural.

High romance brings with it, or seems to bring with it (I'm getting more and more tentative about cause and effect), an expansion of my role here at AMS. I say *role* because doctoring involves you in a kind of cultural performance, the gestures, the lilts, the motions of decent power. It's all okay. Society humors it. I have vacated that nice little office in back there, making way for an older man, and am now more often to be found in the consulting rooms. I don't just do old men anymore. I do women and children too. Even babies. It's as if we can't leave the babies alone. In fact Tod tends to be more upbeat with them here than he is at home (at home, in slippers and dressing gown, longsufferingly shuffling). The babies get wheeled or carried in here, and they're well enough, and you look them over and say something like "This little fella's just fine." And you're always dead wrong. Always. A day or two later the baby will be back, crimson-eared, or whoofing with croup. And you never do a damn thing for them. The challenge, I suppose, is to keep at it while somehow remaining decent.

Then there are the cases that actually entail the strange meeting of man-made glass or metal and human flesh. And human blood. Now this I dependably find a real throw-up number but there's never anything too horrendous because, as my colleagues are always saying, we're at the darning-and-patching level of the biomedical business: the serious cases we bring in direct, and at speed, from the city hospitals, and we in our turn get rid of them as quickly as we

44

can. So you can say this for the maimed and the mangled. They're out of here. Yes, it's quite a deal, at AMS, on Route 6. No wonder people sometimes start right off with an official complaint or even a writ. As for home calls, we refuse over the phone even before we're asked—before we can hear the mother's panic, the baby's cries. We say it's *not our policy*. If you want to get fucked up, you've got to come on over to our place. The money's reasonable. And it doesn't take that long.

Rather as I feared they would, babies have started showing up in Tod's dreams. They've shown up. Or, at least, one of them has. Nothing gruesome happens, and I am coping with it fine so far.

You naturally associate babies with defenselessness. But that's not how it is in the dream. In the dream, the baby wields incredible power. It has the power, the ultimate power of life and death over its parents, its older brothers and sisters, its grandparents, and indeed everybody else who is gathered in the room. There are about thirty of them in there, although the room, if it is a room, can't be much bigger than Tod's nook of a kitchen. The room is dark. More than this, the room is black. Despite the power it wields, the baby is weeping. Perhaps it weeps precisely because of this sinister reversal—the new and desperate responsibilities that power brings. In the faintest of whispers the parents try to give comfort, try to quieten: for a moment it seems that they might even have to *stifle*. There is that excruciating temptation. Because the baby's drastic ascendancy has to do with its voice. Not its fat fists, its useless legs, but its voice, the sounds it makes, its capacity to weep. As usual, the parents have the power of life and death over the baby, which all parents have. Now, though, in these special circumstances and in this special room, the baby has the power

45

over them. And over everybody else who is gathered there. About thirty souls.

The whole thing is a lot tougher on Tod than it is on me. *I'm* always awake when the dreams happen. And I am innocent. . . . The sick shine of imposture and accusation—I don't get that. I know he's only dreaming. I just settle back, with some apprehension, admittedly, and give witness to the late show screened by Tod's head, by his secret mind—by his future. When the time comes to experience the events that Tod's dreams foretell (when we find out, for instance, how the baby came to wield such power), then maybe I will take it harder. Tod himself weeps like a baby before the dreams happen. Occasionally, nowadays, Irene is around to psych him up before he goes in there.

On the TV (look)—on the rooftop, on the ledge, high up, the crying man in the dirty white shirt, holding a baby. Nearby, a policeman, urgently crouched, all cocked and bunched for this urgent encounter or transaction. The cop is saying through his bullhorn that he wants to take the baby. In effect, he wants to disarm the crying man in the dirty white shirt. The crying man has no weapon. The baby is the weapon.

That's not how things stand in the black room, with its groping carbon, its stilled figures. I just know this. In here, the baby is not a weapon. In here, the baby is more like a bomb.

Just when Tod has established our relationship with Irene on a secure footing, the kind of setup that any sane man would kill for, with her punctual visits and affectionate phone calls, the movies we enjoy together, the fine dining, the peace and safety (the forgiveness) that her presence confers, plus the exquisitely torpid lovemaking that takes place right on the button every couple of months or so, and reaching the stage, now, where I think we can tackle her, gently but firmly, about her untidiness around the house, because it's best to get these things out in the open, not to let them rankle and fester, and so on—guess what. Tod has started fooling around. Yeah. With Gaynor.

One Sunday afternoon we took a trancelike ride in the car out to Roxbury, and parked, and strolled the streets, and there she was, standing at her front door in a blue dressing gown with her arms folded and with a look of amused reproach on her face. "You old bastard," she called out. But we got talking to her anyway. I didn't think anything was up until we went inside. Tod, I wanted to say: don't do this. The voice of conscience. It speaks in a whisper. Nobody hears it. One thing led to another—actually it was more like the other way around. After an initial lull we now go out to Gaynor's regularly, every other week.

It's called two-timing, or double-lifting, and that's exactly how it feels. There is integrity-loss. On the other hand it's a buzz physically, I admit, because our new friend has been around quite a bit longer than Irene. This little honey's only fifty-four. But I'm upset. To be frank, I'm scandalized. Last week he went out with *another* one: Elsa. Just lunch, fortunately. It was a very acrimonious occasion and she called us some terrible names. I thought it was a disaster but something tells me that Tod's still hopeful. Is this allowed? I feel as if we're about to get arrested. What's the limit?

Suddenly, to Tod's glands, the world is a woman. Even the sharpness of the city, on a wet night, the veils of rain, the stained darkness—it's a woman. Their shapes are everywhere, and sending messages to his glands. I wonder if Tod's new interest in women is a professional interest, connected

47

to his dealings with them at AMS: his custodial scrutiny of disturbed or distempered female flesh. But his new interest in women seems far too broad and anarchical; it isn't specialized. Unwinding, we sink into the armchair with a coffee cup, and gaze out of the window, and then he'll see an outline across the road (*now* what?), through the fence, through the leaves, and he'll vainly crane and peer, and tip forward onto his feet.

Why? In case it's a woman.

The parallaxes of the stockyards shift and quake. Industry is coming to the city. Gas is cheap. Things move faster than they used to. The insane have been taken off the street; we don't ask where they've disappeared to. Never ask. It's better if you never ask. No longer the nomads, the nightrunners . . . Instead there is a burly altruism abroad. People all have jobs now, at the steel mill and the auto plant. They wash the wind. Just as they clean up all the trash and litter, they also clean up the earth and the sky, transmogrifying cars, turning tools, parts, weapons, bolts, into carbon and iron. They've really got to grips with their environmental problems, facing them squarely, with common purpose. Time for talk is over. There is no talk. Just action. To total sickness you bring total cure. Now there's less room for thought and for feeling, and it seems a great tiredness is good for keeping people steady. Work liberates: Friday evenings, as they move off toward it, how they laugh and shout and roll their shoulders.

Tod loves crowds. In crowds you can be a leader without anyone noticing. Like with the flared pants. He's been sporting those flares of his for quite some time and now everyone is into them. Also the flower shirts and the unctuous neckerchiefs, and that caftan or *dhoti* he dons at weekends—white, and similar in cut to his surgical smock, but with different associations. It's disgusting at his age, I agree, but old people do it and no young people say they can't. Fashion is crowds. Tod wears the red armband too, along with everybody else. Crowds make me paranoid and claustrophobic but Tod seeks and loves the company of crowds. With rapture and relief he elides with the larger unit, the glowing mass. He sheds the thing he often can't seem to bear: his identity, his quiddity, lost in the crowd's promiscuity. My presence is never tinier. But it's the same story. Render up your soul, and gain power.

Under thunderheads, beneath cloudcover like a coated tongue with a doctor's penlight playing on it, as in a dark carnival, we protest the Vietnam War, with vivified, uplifted faces, with the press of bodies all moving the same way, and with that sense of being both lost and right, lost and right. We're half a mile long and young and old and white and black and girl and boy, looking for a monster to kill or create. Signs and banners say the usual things about peace, about war, together with more particular demands like END DE FACTO SEGREGATION and FIRE MRS. AINTREY. Tod stares at FIRE MRS. AINTREY. He doesn't want to fire Mrs. Aintrey. He probably wants to find Mrs. Aintrey—and love her up. He certainly couldn't give two shits about the Vietnam War. Neither is he here, in fairness, just to get women. On the contrary: he's here to get rid of them, to lose them, to drift away from them in the heat and safety of the crowd.

There is another war coming. Oh, yes, we do know that. A big war, a world war, which will roll through villages. It wearies me to imagine the preparations that will prove necessary, what dismantlings and shovelings, what wounds worked open for the sudden closure. . . . There's exactly twenty-five years to go before it starts. That's how come there's so much stuff about it everywhere you look: even everywhere *Tod* looks. I thought for a while that the information would just go on accumulating from here on in, but thank God it's already begun dropping off.

For Tod is highly sensitive to this material. It affects him like a smell, like a chime. Too late . . . There is the same kind of trigger when he hears that other language, not such a rare occurrence now, especially in Roxbury, where he wanders on those Sundays; it is a language in which machines might converse when no human being is around to listen. A third thing makes the trigger slip: nail-clipping. It's the odor the sallow rinds give off, as they cook and crackle in the fire. . . .

I've seen the dates. We're nowhere near young enough for the present war, but when the world war comes—we'll be just right to fight it. We are, after all, a superb physical specimen. Our feet aren't flat. Our vision is clear. We're not clubfooted or Marxist or nuts. We have no conscientious objections or anything of that kind. We're perfect.

The standard affair, nowadays, will start something like this. It starts, in effect, with a moment of *horror*.

Most typically it starts with a late-night drive to some little restaurant. The waiter has just brought us our dough, our honorarium or whatever it is, and we're sitting there quietly snorting and drooling into our brandy balloon, and relishing a perspicacious perfecto. We become aware that people are looking at us. And we don't like it when people are looking at us. . . . Then our eyes will be firmly caught and firmly held by a bent female figure hurrying in through the door and across the room toward us. Fair, dark, slim, plump, elegant, not so elegant. Then she spins round. It's a big power moment when they spin round, with the flourish of challenge, and we get to see what they look like. Speaking personally, for now, it's always cause for alarm, when they spin round—whatever they look like. Because here's the weird thing about these relationships with women: you get everything on the first date. Well, every now and then it's the second date, but generally it's the first. Instant invasion. Instant invasion and lordship. An hour or two here, max, is all it takes. Oh, mercy. You can go up to a woman on a street corner and start yelling at her and ten minutes later she's back at your place doing God knows what. On more than one occasion the first physical contact, the first touch, has been a slap or a shove: the swipe of her hand across Tod's feeble leer of—what? Lust? Contempt? All that needs to happen, in between, is this moment of horror I mentioned. It activates; it legitimates. It seems to be a necessary condition.

So she'll settle at the table, flushed, exalted, imperious, resolute—anyway, thoroughly pissed off—and I'll get the ball rolling with something like,

"Don't go—please."

"Goodbye, Tod."

"Don't go."

"It's no good."

"Please."

"There's no future for us."

Which I greet, I confess, with a silent "Yeah yeah." Tod resumes:

"Elsa," he says, or Rosemary or Juanita or Betty-Jean. "You're very special to me."

"Like hell."

"But I love you."

"I can't look you in the eye."

I have noticed in the past, of course, that most conversations would make much better sense if you ran them backward. But with this man-woman stuff, you could run them any way you liked—and still get no further forward.

51

"Please. You can sleep over."

"This is goodbye, Tod."

"Beth," he'll say. Or Trudy or whatever.

"It just doesn't sit well with me anymore."

"Give me one more chance."

Then they launch into this routine. It lasts from nuts to soup. Don't get them wrong: Tod has his good points. He is, it is widely allowed, "very affectionate" (I think I know what that means. But how would *they* know?). And they don't go on about his obvious flaws, like his being a doctor and having three dozen girlfriends. No, the trouble is, apparently, that Tod can't feel, won't connect, never opens up, always holds something back. What Trudy and Juanita and the rest of them are trying to say, it seems to me, is that Tod gives them the creeps. But whatever it is, whatever it is they're saying or trying to say, it never cramps Tod's style.

He likes to make love in the deathly hour of dusk. He won't let them sleep over—another much-discussed short-coming. Only Irene ever sleeps over. . . . On her lap Beth's handbag yawns. She's miserable that it all has to end. Me, I'm miserable that it's all beginning. By the time we're on the other side of this, I know (I'm experienced), by the time I've become really fond of them and their pretty ways, they will start to recede, irreversibly, fading from me, with the lightest of kisses, the briefest squeeze of the hand, the brush of a stockinged calf beneath the table, a smile. They'll be fobbing us off with the flowers and the chocolates. Oh yes. I've been there. Then, one day, they just look right through you. Next thing you know they switch jobs or cities. All of a sudden they have kids to put through college or they're shacked up with some old wreck of a husband.

Rounding it off with a cocktail, we finish our meal and

sit there doggedly describing it to the waiter, with the menus there to jog our memory. Silence in the car on the way back to his place and the act of love in the hour of dusk. Preceded, as I said, by the moment of horror. And it isn't without its pathetic aspects anyway, this evening scene with the two mature parties, their spectacles, their hair, their heavy old shoes, and the extra trust that she in particular will be needing to feel, and may not feel. Here it comes, like a chime. A naked female stare. Her body is probably naked by now but there is nothing as naked as human eyes: they haven't even got *skin* over them. Like a chime, the moment of intense focus. That same look—full understanding, unwelcome wonder—as if they have just seen everything, even the figure in the dream with his white coat and his black boots and, in his wake, a night sky full of souls. Well, whatever they've seen, it can't bother them all that much. Who knows, it may even work as a kind of sick turn-on. Seconds later they will attest with a sigh to his incredible invasion. And they soon get over it. Thereafter it's no more than a recurrent talking point, or a way of *talking down*, with all this *I don't feel I really* know *you* and *What's really going* on *in there?* and *Show me the* real *you*. The real Tod. Of course, I'm curious too. The real Tod: show me it. But am I sure I really want to watch?

Perhaps Irene puts it best—she certainly puts it most often—when she tells Tod that he has no soul. I used to take it personally, and I was wretched at first. Yet she sticks around. Can Tod be so bad, if she sticks around? She doesn't have to. She's not our mother. . . . Needless to say, Tod has neglected to regale Irene with accounts of his new relationships, his invasions, his conquests, his quiet annexations. But she knows what he's like. She's observant. It was Irene, for instance, who pointed out something I'd never been able to put my finger on: that Tod can't talk and smile at the same time. But maybe he never wants or needs to. . . . He copes okay. With all his ladies and their different bodies, their different odds and ends. Meanwhile, I suffer. I find I am very vulnerable to confusion and regret. If I were given my head, which I never am or will be (for I am impotent. I can make no waves), I would remain faithful to Irene. At least until my wife shows up. It happens to be a matter of principle. One man, one woman: I think we owe this to the human body. I feel like an ardent ghost, like a mute shedding tears of eagerness, as Irene lies in our arms. "Tod may be two-timing," I want to whisper, "but I'm true to you. I am constant. I am true."

In the dream there's always this room, something like a gardener's hut or a potting shed. The implements are wrong. The atmosphere is badly wrong. People are gathered there. It is a room in which something mortal will be monotonously decided.

Tod's hidden mind insists, in dream form, that Tod feels pain. The dreams tell us this in their miserable iteration. And fear. Tod is a big depositor in the bank where fear is kept.

Around midnight, sometimes, Tod Friendly will create things. Wildly he will mend and heal. Taking hold of the woodwork and the webbing, with a single blow to the floor, with a single impact, he will create a kitchen chair. With one fierce and skillful kick of his aching foot he will mend a deep concavity in the refrigerator's flank. With a butt of his head he will heal the fissured bathroom mirror, heal also the worsening welt in his own tarnished brow, and then stand there staring at himself with his eyes flickering.

*   *   *

I have spoken of the three triggers, those stimuli on which Tod's *body* gives judgment. That coppery twang on the emergency cord that hangs tight in his gut. There is a fourth trigger. Like the scorched fingernails, it emanates from fire. Is fire itself a trigger? Fire, which painfully heals and floridly creates out of the slimiest reek and chaos . . .

Once a year the same letter is born from the flames. Tod sits there, direly staring at the grate, and watches the fire's rumor of bared throats and wagging tongues. His larynx gives the complicated click of nausea. Into Tod's mind, of course, I cannot see. But I am the hidden sharer of his body. What's it going through? This: a torment, an outright sepsis of the lowest fear. And relief—ignoble relief. Then the letter unbuckles, turning from black to even white in the heat and delivering itself into our outstretched hand.

The letter always has the same thing to say. Yes, it's rather the kind of correspondence one might expect Tod Friendly to go in for: unvarying, humorless, and one-way, like junk mail. It has this to say:

Dear Tod Friendly: I hope you are well, as we are. It pleases me to inform you that the weather here continues to be temperate!

Yours sincerely. Then the hysterical signature, under which the following name and title is complacently typed: The Reverend Nicholas Kreditor. "Here" (where the weather is ever temperate) is New York, according to the letterhead—more specifically the Imperial Hotel, on Broadway.

And that's it. All the letters get from me is an annual gasp of inanition. But Tod comes on as if New York were next door, and as if temperate weather meant rat showers and devil winds and the mad strobes of Venusian lightning.

He'll sit there by the fire for a long time, with scotch bottle, with alerted chemistry. In the morning, we'll leave the letter on the mat with all the other trash, and it will go away, like Tod's fear.

How will he take it if the weather in New York turns really bad?

It is significant, I am assuming, that nearly all our love affairs come to an end in the consulting rooms of Associated Medical Services. A professional formality prevails as we stand there with one or another of our girlfriends, against a background of height and weight graphs, nutrition rosters, scan and smear tips, and signs saying things like Do You Have Endometriosis? Don't Panic. Nothing much happens, physically, except for some brow-touching and pulse-taking. Oh yes: Tod does his minor violence with the pins: "Any numbing?" Our girlfriends seem to enjoy the charade, at least to begin with; they are flirtatious and collusive. I think it must be Tod's questions that eventually put them off. "How long have you been married?" "Is your husband an active man?" "Do you lead a . . . do you lead a *full* life?" Our girlfriends never lead full lives. They all claim, rather hurtfully, to lead empty ones. Anyway these questions go down like a lead balloon.

Or maybe it's simpler than that, and has to do with their seeing Tod in his natural environment, the doctor, the gatekeeper, with his white coat and his black bag. Our lady friends back out of here forever, with rewritten faces, pausing beyond the closed door and softly knocking, softly knocking, on love's coffin.

Still, there are plenty more where they came from. You find them all over. In the House of the Big One, in Alright Parking, in bars, in doorways on rainy nights, sometimes

scarved and swaddled against the wind and the cold, sometimes naked in strange apartments.

So it's almost total, this immersion in the bodies of others.
And bodies are nice, are they? Is that what I'm supposed to
think? Yes, well, okay—they *are* nice. They forgive everything. When they're old. They can't judge. Irene, whose
white voluminousness forgives everything. She says as
much.

"You don't want to know," Tod whispers in the dark,
before he dreams.

"Whatever it is, I could forgive it."

"You don't want to know," Tod whispers.

She doesn't want to know. *I* don't want to know. No
one wants to know.

And then there is our own body, our own corporeal
instrument, which we're awfully proud of now. The bobbly
briskness of our stride. My, the clarity and attack of our
bowel movements. How perfectly we function. . . . It's
hardly surprising, I suppose, that the ladies go for us in a
big way and come across so quickly, with our impassive
oblong of a face, our clean and powerful hands. If you like
the type, and though I say it myself, Tod *is* incredibly
handsome. . . . This body: his pride in it, I firmly speculate,
is connected to the fear that someone might hurt it—might
mutilate or demolish it. Now why would anyone want to go
and do a thing like that? Doctors may want to; but Tod
doesn't use doctors; he doesn't go near doctors. "You don't
want to listen to doctors," he tells Irene, coming as close as
he ever does to talking and smiling at the same time. "They'll
try to get their knives in you. Don't ever let them get their
knives in you." Sleek and colorful before the mirror in the
bathroom, Tod feels pride that has a wince or a flinch in it.

Go on, I want to say. Mime it out. Bend and cringe with your hands on your loins. Cover your low heart.

Meanwhile I sit in the spacious bar-restaurant, in this drool parlor, in this fancy vomitorium. The woman has come, and now it's meat and tears, with the food growing in heat on our plates. Wait. This one's a vegetarian. She says she loves all animals—but she won't put her money where her mouth is. Soon . . . Jesus, the whole routine is like the very act of lust. First the sadness and disarray, then the evanescent transcendence; then the bodies put on clothes again, and there is a prowl of word and gesture before they go their separate ways.

Tod features another kind of dream in which he is a woman. I'm the woman too: in this dream I am participant as well as onlooker. A man is near us with his face averted, his slablike back half-turned. He can harm us, of course. But he can protect us, if he likes. On his protection we gingerly rely. We have no choice but to love him, nervously. We also have no hair, which is unusual, for a woman. I am delighted to say that we don't see any babies in this dream. We don't see any babies, powerful or otherwise. We don't see any bomb babies, babies with the power of bombs. This dream is childless.

Time is heading on now toward something. It pours past unpreventably, like the reflection on a windshield as the car speeds through city or forest.

Identical twins, dwarves, ghosts, the love lives of Caligula and Catherine the Great and Vlad the Impaler, Nordic iceclouds, Atlantis, the dodo.

Hold on. All of a sudden Tod has started reading travel brochures that praise certain semiremote areas of Canada. Yes, he finds them in the trash. Now Canada is where young men hang out when they really ought to be in Vietnam. Maybe Tod is considering Canada. Maybe Tod is considering Vietnam. Vietnam might do him good. The gibbering hippies and spaced-out fatsoes who go there, they come back looking all clean and sane and fine, after a spell in the war, in the Nam, in what they call *the shit*.

Nicholas Kreditor's latest letter reveals a hidden talent for detail and amplitude. The weather down there in New York, "although recently unsettled," Kreditor writes, "is temperate once more!" I think he's wrong. I think it's changing. I think it's definitely getting stormy.

I knew something was up the minute Tod started selling all the furniture. Throughout the whole process I looked on in wronged silence, like a wife. First every stick of furniture gets carted off, and all my labor-saving appliances, then the carpets and the curtains, if you please. Why was Tod punishing me like this? He got a real kick out of it too, always looking for new ways to uglify the home. On would come the dungarees at the weekend. He prowled around in a simian hunger, searching for things to splatter and deface.

He did a real blitz on the electrics. He took me down for many terrible half hours beneath the floorboards, beneath the joists, with cord or cable in his questing hand; the platonic darkness of this underworld became a figure for our nightlife, candlelit, torchbeam-pierced; our old existence I came to picture as a boundless cathedral of light. He did a similar job on the plumbing. God-awful work, plumbing. Everything's back of everything else; you're all elbows and kneecaps with your cheek crushed against the copper viscera. Anyway, it worked: we now have no water. Just the garden tap. Going to the bathroom these days is quite a heavy trip: the can becomes a kind of geyser, and Tod has to look lively with that bucket of his. Life clangs and swings and scrapes with all these buckets and pails. Until there we are on the bare boards downstairs, with candles and bottled gas and a deli picnic on a paper plate. That's what Tod has brought us to. I mean, when I started out with him I never thought . . . Outside, the defoliated back garden, its bald bush, its sorry grass, its scorched earth.

It wasn't the belt-tightening that depressed me, nor Tod's refractory and sinister cheer, which in any case didn't last long. After all, I am stuck with the old bastard, whatever the lifestyle. It was the solitude growing around me, growing under me: this I couldn't take. The shine of priestly indifference on the faces of shopkeeper and barman. In the eyes of the neighbors a watery oblivion. It's happening at work too now: I can feel it. As for the women—well, thanks, ladies. One by one they stepped out on me. Only Irene persists. She couldn't have been more tactful about the conditions, though her mood was understandably solemn and cautious. Something tells me I won't be seeing her for a while either. Christ, even the dog next door has gone off me, and now hates me. She used to squeeze through the fence and bring me her bones. She used to bounce and romp. Now I get the tensed snarl and the stare of malarial loathing. Bitch. . . . It's like the song says—it's the literal truth. When you're going down, when you're traveling downward through society, then nobody knows you. Nobody knows you.

The evil day came. We moved into a "studio" in Roxbury. I won't describe the room. I can hardly see it anyway, through the mist of my hurt. Well, I hope Tod's happy. . . . He isn't, actually, not anymore. He spends a lot of his leisure, these days, in drunken prayer. The only time he perks up is when we go back to the old house for meetings with the estate agent. The two of them move from room to room and stand there nodding in apparent admiration of Tod's handiwork. The old house—Tod really did a number on it. I don't envy the new tenants. They're hippies or gypsies or squatters or whatever, and they've already started camping out there as best they can. Sorry, guys. What's that little rule about always leaving the bathroom as you'd expect to find it? Well, we played our part, one way or the other. You can't deny that the place is an absolute toilet.

To complete the picture, we now undergo a series of embittering demotions at AMS. One Friday afternoon I hand over my gauzy cream tunic and slip into a kind of butcher's apron, epically and namelessly stained. You could say this for the new position: it took us back a way from the medical cut and thrust. It took us, instead, into the storeroom, the garbage kilns, the pickup truck, and the city dump. This special facility at the city dump, you see: that's where everything comes from. Back in the boiler room with the ten-gallon bags I roll up my sleeves and rummage in heaps of bloody lint and plaster, cracked phials and syringes, crushed cultures. You also get stuff from the incinerator, which I man. Then I divvy up the crap into the rightful pedal bins and trolley them around the building, where nobody knows me. That's who I am, the stained stiff in the industrial gloves. I smell like a major operation. My whole being snags and crackles with broken glass, but that's all right, because although they may smell me, nobody sees me and nobody knows me.

We're as good as invisible now. Perhaps that's the point of this process: the search for invisibility. You find it, invisibility, for a while, in a crowd, or behind the closed door of the bathroom (where, during that heavy transaction, by common consent, everybody is invisible), or in the deed of love; or it can be found down here, where you are unknown. Jo, my collaborator in disposal (old, fat, black, and stationary, glued to the heat of the incinerator: "Hey!" "Yo!" "Jo!" "Hey!"), he knows me. And Dr. Magruder will sometimes glitter potently in my direction as I make the rounds. Friendless Friendly. We move with no friction, head down, staring at the floor. We're definitely on the way out.

Is it that the human being is secretly nothing without others? He disappears. Even Jo has started looking at me oddly, as if I'm not quite there. The only body we have now is our own. And if we're wicked and shouldn't be seen, why are we becoming more beautiful?

I'm on a train now, heading south at evening. The American Atlantic moves past me. All business is concluded. I don't know where we're going: our ticket, dispensed with a contemptuous flick by the station trash can, bears the name of our starting point, not our destination. I feel that something similar applies to me and Tod, to our identity. "Tod Friendly," Tod Friendly keeps grunting without opening his mouth, as if he's trying to remember it, or learn it. Our pitiful impedimenta: one uncarriably heavy suitcase full of clothes and money and our human remains; and one body clotted with rotten adrenaline. Tod's heart cowers like an oyster at any quick movement from the other bodies in our car. Transports of heart and train . . . Shit, here comes the serge shoulderspan of the guard, his neck bent in judgment. He dots my ticket and moves away with an interrogatory stare. Oh, we really don't feel so good. Maybe it would be better if we sat facing the other way? The train says Tod Friendly Tod Friendly Tod Friendly . . .

Stop it. Stop the train! I somehow thought I was in a state of full ordeal readiness. Ready for continued descent—

but on a modest gradient. Jesus, my poor bourgeois dreads: another undesirable residence, perhaps, more low company (if any), or possibly (I had faced this, with martyred mien) the life of the open road. But come *on*. Tod's glands are in their dream mode, whinnying in nightmare. So maybe these are the things we're heading toward: the white coat and the black boots, the combustible baby, the soiled bib on its hook, the sleet of souls. The wooden room where something lethal will be lugubriously decided. Everybody dreams about being harmed. It's easy. Much tougher to recover from the dream of harming . . . America swipes by the window, cattle, timber, wheat, offerings from a younger world. With rushing eagerness I look for calm—to the ocean, not its nervous surface and its frayed edges, but the hidden depth to which everything is eventually returned.

It must be New York. That's where we're going: to New York and its stormy weather.

He is traveling toward his secret. Parasite or passenger, I am traveling there with him. It will be bad. It will be bad, and not intelligible. But I will know one thing about it (and at least the certainty brings comfort): I *will* know *how* bad the secret is. I will know the nature of the offense. Already I know this. I know that it is to do with trash and shit, and that it is wrong in time.

3

Because I am a healer, everything I do heals

This business with the yellow cabs, it surely looks like an unimprovable deal. They're always there when you need one, even in the rain or when the theaters are closing.

They pay you up front, no questions asked. They always know where you're going. They're great. No wonder we stand there, for hours on end, waving goodbye, or saluting—saluting this fine service. The streets are full of people with their arms raised, drenched and weary, thanking the yellow cabs. Just the one hitch: they're always taking me places where I don't want to go.

Our first thirty-six hours in New York were hectic but not frightening. They seemed to have to do with our identity. Getting a new one. Or getting rid of the old one. We also had to settle in at the new apartment, which I'm very impressed by (and only hope it's a long let, but I'm scatter-brained about such things and leave all that to Tod). Or better say "Tod." Tod won't be Tod for much longer. He'll trade in that name and get a better one. See you, Tod. . . . Then, too, we made the acquaintance of Nicholas Kreditor. I wouldn't claim to know how it all added up. Anyway, I set it down, I lay it out. I sometimes feared for myself, at first, but not for others. This is what happened to us when we came to New York.

We eased in under the city: Grand Central, where the train sighed, and the passengers sighed, one by one. The first people to leave went off hastily, while others lingered, girding themselves for the streets. Tod held his head down for a couple of minutes, then sloped off. Among the shadows of the platform he kept wrenching his neck around—for the first time in his life he seemed to be trying to look where he was going. As a result he kept bumping into everybody. His bows, his flourishes, his veronicas of apology. He jumped the queue at the ticket counter—his stub realized eighteen dollars—but went on standing there in line, his head baby-ishly lolling with impatience, before he peeled off into the store-flanked tunnels. Outside, the cab pulled up smartly, as they do. And we were traveling again, through ravine, under totem. Why not begin, I thought nervously, with a visit to the Empire State Building or the Statue of Liberty? But that would have been *very* old-fashioned. It was November. The humans had grown their winter coats, and the high buildings trembled in the tight grip of their stress equations.

The new apartment consisted of a single room the size of a small warehouse: solid-wood desk and table, low-slung black leather chairs, filing cabinets, the playpen of the bed. Unlike our previous habitats, it had personality. It was butch. Unsmiling, hygienic, and butch. The man who lived here would have definite elixir theories about his yogurts, his knee bends, his nudist vacations. Well—whatever—now's the time, one would have thought, for Tod and me to kick off our shoes and get the feel of the place. But no. We had our own personality question to straighten out. And in the second cab, heading east, seeing the personnel, those who are faceless, and those who are *all* face, all hair and gesture, I wondered if everyone needed new identities when they came to New York. Or was it just us. Just him. Not "Tod," not any longer. The name on the bell, the name on the door, the name on the envelopes under the table lamp: they said John Young, John Young, John Young. Scraps of paper, issuing from the city, came twirling in through the cab window. We healed them with our doctor's hands and placed them about our person. Letters, membership cards, bills, receipts. All said John Young. What else was out there? Cars, of course. Of course cars. Cars, cars, cars, as far as the eye could see.

Next stop was the ID parlor, the identity basement, deep down, and hard on the senses, with that sharp dry-cleaner heat and, further back, the padded shunting, the press and release of enslaved machinery. We dealt with a wised-up kid, a specialist, an urban idiot savant, who wore a thimblelike monocle. At one point, early on, this kid was counting out money and saying something like, you haven't got a choice there and if you don't like it you can shop around, when we said, in a voice I'd never heard before, a voice that no longer pretended to be nice, a voice that expressed all the effort of pretending to be nice for so long,

" 'Tod Friendly'? What the fuck kind of name is that?"

"There," said the kid. "Clean."

We had to keep going away and coming back again. The basement stall got harder and harder to find our way out of. We tried to eat. We fished stuff out of the trash cans in Washington Square Park, a sandwich, an apple intact but for the missing bite, then to the Superette for nickels and dimes. Time passed. Time, the human dimension, which makes us everything we are. Until this final exchange.

"Well then," we said, with perhaps inappropriate bitterness, as the kid handed over our new papers, plus a whole ton of money. "I'm at your mercy."

"Double," he said.

"You tell me."

"I hope he told you how it goes on this same-day shit. At a weekend."

"Good."

"Yeah. From the Reverend."

"You're expecting me. My name is John Young."

And that was it. My name is John Young.

The longest day, it really was the longest day ever. Already the train ride seemed years distant, like Wellport, like old age. But John Young couldn't sleep. With its sounds of many cars and few birds, dawn faded. And John Young lay there, wanting fear to be over. Over . . . I thought of the chess players in the park, where we sat for so many hours, the chess players, more various by far than the pieces they wielded (the players not erect, not regulated, but mumbling, shambling, rhomboid). Each game, it's true, begins in disarray and goes through episodes of contortion and cross-purpose. But things work out. All that scowl and elbow and tenseness of posture, all that agony—it works out. One final tug on the white pawn, and perfect order is restored; and the players at last look up, smiling and rubbing their hands. Time will tell, and I put my trust in time, absolutely. As do the chess players, of course, every move legitimated by the slapped clock.

Thank God. He's out. Like a baby. Though naturally I'm still here: even in the darkness I keep a watch upon the world. Sometimes—now, for instance—I look down on Tod, on John, as a mother might (mother night), and try to find hope in the innocence or neutrality of his sleep.

So now we wake up a new man. John Young. Johnny Young. Or how about *Jack* Young? I kind of like it. Ho hum. Feeling no pain suddenly. Reach out here (whoops) for a cleansing few gulps of . . . Jesus. Wild Turkey.

Our clothes came at us from all over the room. A shoe like a heavy old bullet thrown out of the shadows, and skillfully caught, off-balance and one-handed; windmilling trousers trapped by the foot and then kicked up onto the leg; that serpent necktie. I got a very bad feeling as we pitched into the bathroom and fumbled for the mouthwash. Then we knelt before the altar of the can—and pulled the handle. The bowl filled with its terrible surprises. Oh, man. We've done this once or twice before, as I vividly recall. It seems to me about the most you can ask of the human body. Now we solaced our brow on the porcelain, and emitted a few sour gasps of disgust. And got down to it. The premise for alcohol abuse, one gathers, is that consciousness, or selfhood, or corporeality, is intolerable. But it *is* intolerable. Certainly when you're chockful of gangrene. Here it comes again, consciousness, weary, multiform, intolerable.

We went out into New York City and staggered here and there through the Village and drooled it all out in bar after bar. They wouldn't serve us at the first few joints we tried, which wasn't surprising, because we came through the door yelling our head off, or trying to, in this faulty new voice of ours. There was, I remember, quite a restful interlude up some alley or other, during which we reclined panting on a heap of cardboard boxes; then two young men jovially gathered us up and escorted us back into the action. Next we went to see what the hell was going on in a couple of places farther down the block. I can understand why John was overexcited by New York, where, at night, life and all its color and reflection is folded out onto the street, and not shut in and huddled, behind the glow of windows. In any event by six o'clock he was in okay shape. Outside the last bar the cab was waiting remorselessly, the driver with his face averted, waiting to take me somewhere I didn't want to go.

Like the driver I knew where we were going without being told. The fireman's ladder of Seventh Avenue, climbed on the rungs of the cross streets, uptown, then the swinging rope of Broadway. This must be Nicholas Kreditor, our weatherman, and the Imperial Hotel.

The man, the Reverend, was big, handsome, sad, and powerful. He had the snouty, screen-filling face of a politician. Not that he'd ever get anywhere with it, in the U.S., not these days anyway. The coloring was wrong, the tango-tutor's mustache was wrong. I thought instantly that there was something pathetic and obscene about his thick burgundy suit, which made you wonder what other kinds of outfit or uniform he'd like to dress up in. His black necktie was steadied by a gold pin the shape of a crucifix. There were other religious accessories around the place and, on the walls, idealized renderings of New Testament scenes. We sat facing him from the customer's end of a leather-topped desk. Sinisterly, there were two beds in this inner room, twin beds, with identical coverlets and cushion arrangements.

For a while he talked details, addresses, some familiar, some not. Then he said,

"I just want to make clear that I pay you every correctitude for what you were involved in over there."

John said gratefully, "All I ever wanted to do was help people."

"You'll be able to continue with your fine work. I guarantee it."

He guaranteed it. With his limp shrug. The Imperial was full of old people. It was an old-people hotel. We had seen and sensed them on our way up, their tentative postures, their unanimity of hesitation. Judging by his office suite, and his strictly localized charisma, I assumed that the old people were partly in Kreditor's care. *I guarantee it. . . .* You could imagine him guaranteeing a lot of things, or at least saying he guaranteed things a lot.

John said, "I do want to go on helping people."

"Make a clean break and resume elsewhere. It's another plus you have no family."

"That's necessary?"

"Better yet," he said, "just leave New York. Thus far in it's all at state level. We're not talking San Cristóbal. We're talking New Jersey. We're not even talking Canada."

"That I don't need."

"Our backup could take the form of a defense fund and legal help."

"What do you advise?"

71

"The Immigration and Naturalization Service. To revoke your citizenship."

"Explain."

"Worst case: the Justice Department makes an application to the INS."

The Reverend paused. "God forbid," he said, and touched his cruciform tiepin with a buxom fingertip. For a moment, again, he looked sad and powerful. The sadness, perhaps, of the intercessor or shaman who, though in close and constant touch with the spirit world of angels and demons, is often oppressed by the thought of his own talent-lessness—when set against their virtues and glamours, their hoodoos, their evil eyes.

"The only present danger," Kreditor resumed, "is if the press pick up on it like they did with that poor, poor lady in Queens."

John waited. He was staring at the twin beds. Then, both quickly and suddenly, he turned to the Reverend—who was now holding before him a photograph, of which he allowed us only the briefest glimpse. Thank Christ. This photograph, this swipe of grain, so briefly glimpsed: I could tell it contained extraordinary information. It was black and white. It was about power. Twelve men were depicted there, in unmistakable configuration. Twelve men, but two distinct human types, equally represented, six of one type, half a dozen of the other. The first type had power, and safety in numbers. The second type had no power—had numbers, but no safety: numbers conferred only grief and weakness. The first type was silently saying something to the second type. Six men were saying to the other six: Whatever else divides us, whatever else is between us, only one thing matters. We belong to the living, you to the dead. We are the living and you are the dead. The dead.

"So. All they have is this, which is thirty years old, and two so-called witnesses."

"Nothing," said John.

"What, nothing?"

"I *had* no criminal record."

"The usual catch: did you lie about your criminal record?"

"Ah."

"It's taking the form of inquiries about your U.S. naturalization."

"Go on."

"There's some heat," said Kreditor.

And I wondered if he meant the heat that was all over John's body. Now John looked away shyly and said, "My mother . . ."

Kreditor seemed interested. "That's a plus for us."

"My first language."

"Hey, that's right, I remember. You're the one with no accent."

The two men stood up and shook hands. John said,

"I'm going to tell you the truth. Yesterday was better."

"Sir, how are you today?"

"Reverend."

"Doctor."

John and I returned to our new home, but it was difficult, at first, to take any pleasure in the place (the vast skylight, for example), John's state being what it was. It would have been nice to be able to keep out of his way. A woman, someone like Irene, I know, would have found him horrible to be near. So you can imagine what he was like to be inside.

Then the Reverend called, with his news about the weather turning stormy, and I thought he was the last person we needed to hear from. But after that, well, it was all sea breezes. The afternoon passed in happy loneliness, TV, newspaper, the inspection of various little perplexities: waste disposer, toenail, shirt button, light bulb. Consciousness *isn't* intolerable. It is beautiful: the eternal creation and dissolution of mental forms. Peace . . . As noon approached John adopted a behavior pattern that I knew well: stretching, scratching, complacently sighing. It meant that he was about to go to work.

I could only watch as he changed. The short-sleeved bib, the white smock. I looked for the black boots. No. Just the white clogs. What hope from them? John was purged now, and fully awake to the world.

As he walked the five blocks no one tried to stop him. The heavens didn't weep above his head, nor did the fat-cheeked clouds assume sneers of calamity. Likewise the ground, the concrete, which did not cleave to devour or entomb him. And the wind ditto, smoothing past in sweet-zephyr form, no devil-breath, no hurricano. I could adduce only the hopeless weeping of a child, the terrified stare of a black bum on Thirteenth and Seventh, and the way all the walkers, city-users, the tragedians of the street—the way they all seemed to be fleeing, and the uniformed ones (those that are responsible) saying, *Don't mind us. We just wreck buildings* or *We just start fires* or *We just scar highways* or *We just spread trash.* Here is the building, with doormen, porters, receptionists, wheeling caterers, hurrying stretcher-bearers, who know who we are. Dr. Young. For we, we, we!—we demolish the human body.

At such times, I conclude, the soul can only hang in the dark, like a white bat, and let darkness have the day. Beneath, the body does what it does, in mechanical exertions of will and sinew, while the soul waits. It must be safe to assume—surely to God—that *this is it*. This is the gravamen of the dreams of Tod Friendly, of John Young, where the half-dead stand in line and a white-coated figure sweats with power, cruelty, and beauty, with all that is entirely unmanageable. But the dreams lied. I thought (I was sure) that our transgression would be some kind of departure. I thought it would be extraterritorial, out of society, forming its own new universe. I certainly never figured Tod/John for a *life* of crime. And yet it turns out to be the same old stuff only worse, more, again, further. I mean, where is the limit? Show me the ultimate intensifiers of sin. What can you categorically *not* do to someone else's body? I won't claim ignorance. Pretty much the same sort of shit was coming down at AMS, if we'd gone looking for it, and of course it was happening all over town at well-known locations: St. Mary's, St. Andrew's, St. Anne's. It is general. It is general hospital. Nobody can pretend for a minute that they don't know what's going on. The ambulance is out there screaming for all to hear, its lights looping, lassoing: watch us hog-tie all the horrors of the night. Behind the fringe of orange crime-scene tape, on the street, the chalked outline of a human body. Here we are in our fatigues, delivering our damage. Stand back! People—don't interfere. Let us do what we need to do.

The air of the hospital is lukewarm, and it hums, and tastes of human organs obscurely neutralized or mistakenly preserved. We the doctors move between ceiling and floor, between striplight and the croak of linoleum. In these passages there is a feeling of necessary novocaine; morally we are like the refrigerated tongue on the dentist's chair, mouth open as wide as it ever goes to the instruments of pain, but speechless. In the operating room you can only see my eyes.

Here the men cover their hair with paper caps, the women with scarves. On my feet are wooden clogs. Clogs. Why clogs? I wear my surgical gown, my skintight rubber gloves. I wear an outlaw's mask. My headlight band is connected to a transformer on the floor, half-submerged in blood. The cord goes down my back, under my surgical gown, and wiggles around behind me, like tail of monkey, tail of fiend. With our eyes we see only the eyes of the others there. The victim is invisible, fully shrouded: except for the bit we're working on. When it's over, we wash our hands like trained neurotics. The printed sign on the mirror enjoins: Each Finger Nail Should Be Stroked Fifty Times. Finger Tips Should Be Kept Higher Than Elbows. Each Stroke Requires Two Motions. Each Finger Has Four Sides. Then the fluorescence of the locker room, its cord carpet and steel shelves, the laundry barrels and the fattest trash cans you ever saw, from which we fish our presmeared tackle. Out in Casualty it's always Saturday night. Everything is possible.

You want to know what I do? All right. Some guy comes in with a bandage around his head. We don't mess about. We'll soon have that off. He's got a hole in his head. So what do we do? We stick a nail in it. Get the nail—a good rusty one—from the trash or wherever. And lead him out to the Waiting Room where he's allowed to linger and holler for a while before we ferry him back to the night. Already we're busy with this bag lady we've got, welding sock and shoe plastic onto the soles of her evil feet. . . . When we're done with the bad ones, we can't wait to get them out of here. *Gangway*. It doesn't matter. There's always more.

I keep thinking I know them. This happens ten times a day. I keep thinking I know them, these that are wheeled on trolleys or borne on stretchers. Wait. Wasn't that Cynthia, who worked in the deli? Was that woman maybe

76

Gaynor, whom I knew with the act of love? But surely this is Harry, the doorman at the Met. It all happens so fast. I can't hear, with the screams and the ribcrack. Whose child is that? Wasn't he the kid who used to dash across the road, back in Wellport? So many years. Slow. Children.

But then again our world is suddenly very full, humanly, full of faces and voices. Everybody knows me. I am not referring to the victims, of course, who don't know me and who, for all practical purposes, aren't human but come in sections of interest, so that even their smiles and yawns and frowns come in sections. (This habit I have of thinking I know them—as humans—is mistaken, and inappropriate. I don't know them.) I know everybody else. For the first time in my life I have friends, and interests, shared interests, like baseball and opera and partying, and I gleam and bobble with privilege. All these strangers know me. From the outset the whole team here at the hospital was instinctively pally and collegial. Esprit de corps is first rate, even idealistic. The thing called society—it's behind us. We mediate between man and nature. We are soldiers of a sacred biology. Because I am a healer, everything I do heals, somehow. The thing called society is, I believe, insane. In the locker room the steel grills are pasted with letters that say, Thanks for your kindness for making a tough time much easier to bear, and If it wasn't for all of you there at the hospital I don't know how we would have survived. The doctors read these thank-you notes with tears in their eyes, especially when gratitude is expressed in a childish hand. Not Johnny Young, though. Perhaps he knows, as I do, that the letters are propitiatory. The children ("7 yrs") haven't been here yet. They won't be so grateful when we're through.

We have many hobbies (life has filled up and fanned out), but our main extracurricular interest, naturally, is women's bodies. Women's bodies, which Johnny finds so much more interesting, by so many magnitudes, than everything else put together. He isn't after women's bodies for only one thing, not Johnny. He is after women's bodies for all the other things too: love, spiritual communion, loss of self, exaltation. Women's bodies bring out all his finer feelings. The fact that a woman's body has a head on top of it isn't much more than a detail. Don't get me wrong: he needs the head, because the head wears the face, and supplies the hair. He needs the mouth; he badly needs the mouth. As for what the head contains, well, yes, Johnny needs some of the things that live in there: will, desire, perversity. To the extent that sex is in the head, then Johnny needs the head.

Originally I was going to adopt a distant and defeated tone. Something like: As for John's sexual life during our years here in the city, suffice it to say that he dated a lot of nurses. But it doesn't suffice. Saying something like that never does suffice. It's true about nurses, by the way. Or it's true about the nurses John dates, and they seem to be a pretty typical crowd. The work looks like hell to me, it looks like loin-death from where I'm sitting, but hospitals are erotic—that's what they all say. They're always ribbing one another about it. Blood and bodies and death and power. I suppose you can see the connection. They are reconciling themselves to their own mortality. They are doing what we all have to do down here on earth: they are getting ready to die. Thus, for Dr. Young, the fatal, the mortal, the life-deciding interest in women's bodies. What can it be about women's bodies, apart from their being so incredibly interesting?

There is a fire-tinge of violence to it here in New York, as there is to everything in this city, which just won't slow down like the other city did and get more innocent and less crazy and less dirty-colorful. It makes our earlier romancing—where love would sadly bloom in a parking lot or with bitter words before a shop window dribbling with rain—seem downright courtly. For instance. He gets up at two in the morning and ventures out for a stroll. We're on Sixth Avenue, puffing on a prosaic perfecto and minding our own business—when John turns down Twenty-second Street, breaks into a run, and starts loosening his pants. . . . *Now* what? Those pants of his were around his knees when he slammed through the double doors of the brownstone, and around his ankles as he stumbled at speed up the first flight of stairs. We hopped straight into this apartment, straight into the bright bedroom—and turned. I have to say that the situation didn't look very promising. There was a woman in the bed, right enough. But there was a man there too. Fully clothed, enormous in midnight-blue serge suit and peaked cap, he knelt above her, rhythmically slapping her face with a pendulum action of his heavy-gloved hand. No, this didn't look like our kind of thing at all. Warily John slipped out of his socks and shirt. You have to give him credit: he keeps his cool and works the percentages. Now the two men moved strangely past each other; and with some diffidence John climbed into bed. The other guy stared at us, with raised, with churning face. Then he did some shouting and strode out of there—though he paused, and thoughtfully dimmed the lights, as he left the room. We heard his boots on the stairs. The lady clutched me.

"My husband!" she explained.

Who cared? Instantly John invaded her. With zero foreplay. No hair-stroking or sighing or staring sorrowfully at the ceiling, not for her. No extra-loud snoring or anything, not for this baby. . . . Soon afterward she took up a position at the hospital. Nurse Davis. We still date. Her husband,

Dennis, is a nightwatchman. She keeps saying she's glad Dennis doesn't know about us and she hopes he never finds out. What is it with them, the human beings? I suppose they remember what they want to remember. And I suppose, in our case, John and I should exchange high fives in squalid thanks to this human talent for forgetting: forgetting, not as a process of erosion and waste, but as an activity. John forgets. Nurse Davis forgets. The husband, Dennis, shuddering in the cold on his way to work, on his way to watch the night, forgets.

Largely out of a sense of duty I search for connections between the two interests, between the two kinds of female body. One body wallows on a barge of pillows, with warmly tousled gaze and smelling of fresh bread (you'll get no argument from me there: women *are* great); the other body lies flat and cold on a table down whose eaves blood runs, like a sunset. John attends them both with his animal parts thickened. Here's another one, he seems to think. Another face with its bridal train of hair. Another thigh of astonishing might. Another female belly.

With the children, at the hospital, in Pediatrics, where the light is never off, where the little victims whom we patiently deform lie drugged and lost and itching—with the children John is at his briskest. He surges through the wards snatching toy and lollipop, wearing a skull's smile. No feeling tone. Only the men get to him. Funnily enough. He meets their eyes with a look that almost confesses. Confesses that they have a right which he hereby violates. And what is this right? It is the right to life and love.

With the men, the doctor's cultural performance is at its most tenuous. It is abruptly open to question, this idea the doctors hold in secret, that they must wield the special power; because if the power remains unused, then it will become unmoored, and turn back against their own lives.

Carter was an exception, to this and to everything else, but I used to feel that I was roughly the same age as the reigning American president. People said I resembled Gerry Ford, though of course I'm a lot more handsome than that now. I was younger than LBJ, at least to start with, and I'm definitely older then JFK, who's even handsomer than I am. JFK: flown down from Washington and flung together by the doctors' knives and the sniper's bullets and introduced onto the streets of Dallas and a hero's welcome.

Now despite years of steady disarmament they're all talking about nuclear war again, and more intensely than ever before. I wish I could put their minds at rest. It isn't going to happen. Come on: imagine the preparations that would be needed. No one's even started. No one's ready.

Remember the punks? They were ready. The experiments in mortification they performed on their own faces—the piercings, the pallor. The punks had made a start. They were ready. But they vanished decades ago.

Here's a little moment I'd like to share.

I'm in the waiting room of the Peter Pan Ward, shooting the breeze with Nurse Judge. There is another woman there, a Mrs. Goldman. Because she is a woman, John glances at her from time to time: because she is a woman. But she is also a mother: she has a baby at her feet, and a further child, a three-year-old girl, whose hips we have decided to destroy. The girl is lying in the Peter Pan Ward with her lower half in plaster. She's been there for months—it's a long-term project. . . . Mrs. Goldman is reading a magazine, with the baby at her feet. We've seen this pair before. The baby is shrinking fast, and can't really crawl now though its struggles are something to see. But wait a minute. The baby *is* crawling, only one or two panting inches at a time—but crawling *forward*. And the mother with the magazine, the glossy pages ticking past her face: she's reading, or skimming, *forward*. Hey! Christ, how long has it been since I . . . ? Anyhow, it's soon over, this lucid interval. The mother is reading backward again, and the baby is merely weeping. It wants its diaper changed, or it's hungry. It wants its diaper filled, with new shit from the trash. I'm being immature. I've got to get over it. I keep expecting the world to make sense. It doesn't. It won't. Ever.

You have to harden your heart to pain and suffering. And quick. Like right away at the very latest.

We couldn't get through half an hour of this without the necessary conditions, humanly. We're real antic about it. Among the tepid metal and tile of the locker room, or slumped over the paper cups and coffee balloons of the commissary—Johnny's there, with unspeakable skid marks all over his smock. Our victims we call stiffs and slabs and sides—and fuck-ups, and organ donors.

"Not like the blob. You see the blob?"

"Ah, she ain't so bad off."

"You see the splat case?"

It isn't much, but I'll say this for Dr. John Young. He takes no pleasure in his work. The self is a muffled self: it wears a suit of protective clothing. This despite the overtime he voluntarily puts in. Opinions of him vary: he is "incredibly dedicated"; he is "a glutton for punishment"; he is a "saint"; he is "a fucking maniac." "Well," says John, and shrugs lightly, "you do what you do best."

Johnny is stronger than the other doctors, the brothers,

the sisters. They're forever faltering, rocking on their platforms. Johnny needs no encouragement—but he gives it. Here's Byron, who looks like Bluto, with his breadth of black beard, and body hair sprouting luxuriantly through his shoulder laces.

"Talk to me, Byron."

"Johnny, look at me, I'm losing it."

"Who told you it was going to be easy?"

"I'm not up to this shit."

And so on. It never helps. They're in far worse shape, as always, when John's done. Byron rocks away, very hairy, very clean, wringing his hands, like an impeccable spider in his green fatigues.

And the body beneath is so tired all the time. It never ends. I work a lot with Witney. Witney? Thirty-two, tall, rubber-lipped, pop-eyed, very smart but no culture so just wised-up: that's Witney. He thinks he's cool; he talks about Korea, and how, compared to that, this is nothing. No big deal. There was this incident with Witney when, I don't know—oh yeah. We'd just totaled a couple of teenage boys. Their mothers had brought them in and then got the hell out soon after we started work, staying only to witness the methodical unraveling of the soaked bandages. We took the stitches out and swabbed the boys with blood. I remember Witney's skillful insertion of some kind of crossbow bolt; me, I was wedging shards of brown glass into the other boy's crown. And we both, as they say, *cracked up:* we laughed at each other, full face, showing at last with teeth and tongue and tonsils the mortal hilarity that sniggers behind everything we do here. Our laughter, together with the boys' cries and whimpers. Oh yeah. And Witney goes, to my one, "Expecting a break-in, kid? You look like a garden wall." Or something like that, which seemed to calm us both, as jokes

83

will. Humor keeps you steady, after all, even when the shit's coming down. Our hilarity contained terror, of course it did, terror of our own fragility. Our own mutilation. Who might commit it? How can we avert it? Soon Witney and I were busy elsewhere with hacksaw and medium chisel, attaching a farcically mangled leg to an unknown and shrouded figure, at the thigh, in a kind of rain of blood, a snow of bone.

The city—it is the city that will have to heal them, with knifeblade and automobile, nightstick, gunshot. The local passions of love and hate. The loose cables and rogue masonry of the telekinetic city.

There is the Laundry Room on the second floor, scene of trysts and quickies and what the team here call *knee-tremblers*, which is when you do it standing up. I have been there with Nurse Davis. I now go there with Nurse Tremlett.

There are two Recovery Rooms on the fourth floor where it's usually okay. I used to go there with Nurse Cobretti. I hope to go there soon with Nurses Sammon and Booker. Sometimes I don't even bother to take off my gown, which is all smeared and tiretracked. I just kick off my clogs.

There is a nurse called Nurse Elliott who is always sneering at me without meeting my eye. In the elevator yesterday, under her breath, she called me an asshole. I know the signs—when a woman is leading me on. She's just slipped into the Laundry Room. After a minute or two I follow her through the door. She stands by the window, checking her face in the silver compact. I walk toward her with my knees trembling.

John will look in on these nurses after hours in their studios and boardinghouses, in their chambers and parlors, but it's only the very special nurses who in any way establish themselves at his attractive address. With the very special nurses

John adopts a markedly different amatory style. This style I would designate as above all *thorough*. You could say it's a return to his earlier mode, but ramified by increased stamina. There is a kind of duty roster of the things he needs to do. All that can be done will be done—generally right away, too. He seems to search their bodies. He seems to search their bodies, for undivulged openings, new incisions.

And guess who's started showing up, intermittently to begin with but now on a twice-monthly basis. Irene. John took it coolly enough, but for me it was the tenderest agony, particularly at first. And the funny thing is: I thought I was more or less over Irene. I hadn't been thinking about her that much, just a few times a day, and seldom imagined that I'd glimpsed her here or there on the street, on a bus, in the Superette, in the hospital, on a passing airplane five miles high. Over Irene? Fine chance. Maybe you're doomed in the heart, as they say, and you're never over your first love. And then this nightmare complication: I can't *stand* the way he treats her. To him she is—how can I put this?—soon assimilated. She is instantaneously assimilated. The tiredest glance, the flattest smile assimilates her. It's an impossible situation. John isn't *thorough* with Irene. She should get so lucky. It's one of those triangular things. I love her but she loves him and he loves no one. At night she lies there blinking with neglect. John lies folded over the other way. I *burn* for her.

The years have been kind to Irene, though she's still a lot more tired and worn than even the roughest of our nurses. I note this, and harp on her imperfections, as a defense mechanism. Yes, I am always hopelessly trying to poison myself against her. She could certainly be tidier around the apartment, which is usually so spick-and-span when she arrives. I'm at one with John on this. We do abhor dust and dirt, and stains on the bathtub, and any kind of filth.

Time passes. Cars are fatter and fewer, and imitate animals with their fins and wings.

Syringes are no longer disposable. At the hospital there's generally a greater emphasis on make-do and catch-as-catch-can. We even use pipettes: *so* unhygienic. And they've phased out cottonoid, which is a drag.

The standing of doctors in society is higher than ever. We walk tall, no longer cowed by writs.

You don't see cyclists wearing those doctor's masks. There are no more warnings, on polleny days, for asthmatics and hay-fever sufferers.

Everyone smokes and drinks and messes around. No one works out.

Last week they came and took away my color TV. They gave me a black-and-white one. I made on the deal, but when I switched it on my first thought was: uh-oh. There goes world opinion.

But world opinion, as a force, went long ago, really. You can't say exactly when it happened. After the moon shot, I remember, a little light went out in everybody's head; suddenly the world seemed cozier, more local, fuggier. World opinion, on the other hand, disappeared slowly. Like dental self-consciousness. You see ogreish smiles all over the place these days, and nobody minds. People don't mind so much what other people are like. So people can be what they are, not minding if others mind.

Clothes everywhere become more innocent. Everyone becomes more innocent, constantly forgetting. Central Park is cleaner but no safer. We are fewer.

Picture me now in the operating room, on the black tile floor, under the kettle lights, with a mild headache and half a hard-on, spooning tumor into the human body. I rest for a moment, availing myself of the leather bike seat on its stiff chrome stand. The scrub nurse, Nurse del Puablo, is giving me the eye. This is all she can give me, in her surgical yashmak. I have slept with her. So have Byron and Witney. Nurse del Puablo is widely and justly celebrated for her skilled hands, hot thighs and soft lips, her pretty belly, bad ass and *good* tits.

I want to get this tumor packed in nice and firm. I say, "Bayonet . . . Mosquito . . . Sucker . . . Clamp."

At night the hospital creaks and ticks with cullings and triage.

On their final date, John and Nurse del Puablo went to the Metropolitan Museum. John doesn't care for the paintings, and there's no financial incentive, but he feels that it's expected of him, by nurses, and by the stone and metal hydra called society. Like writing, paintings seem to hint at a topsy-turvy world in which, so to speak, time's arrow moves the other way. The invisible speedlines suggest a different nexus of sequence and process. That thought again. It always strangely disquiets me. I wonder: is this the case with all the arts? Well, it's not the case with music. It's not the case with opera, where everyone walks backward and sounds god-awful.

Every Christmas we get a card from the Reverend, informing us that the weather is temperate. Well, sometimes it is and sometimes it isn't. But I know what he means.

The hospital is like a permanent November. One walks through sun and rain, one walks through all kinds of weather to get there, but once sucked inside by the blatting doors, everything is desperately and essentially gray. Through these windows, at evening, the clouds look like bandages and cottonoid.

All the intelligent pain of the victims, all the dreams of the unlistened to, all the entreating eyes: all this is swept up in the fierce rhythm of the hospital.

"You do good work, Doctor," everyone here tells me. I deny this. I immolate myself in denial. If I died, would he stop? If I am his soul, and there were soul-loss or soul-death, would that stop him? Or would it make him even freer?

I am not fond of these paradoxes, if paradoxes they are; and I don't expect everybody—or indeed anybody—to see it my way. But you can't end yourself, not here. I am familiar with the idea of suicide. Once life is running, though, you can't end it. You're not at liberty to do that. We're all here for the duration. Life *will* end. I know exactly how long I've got. It looks like forever. I feel unique and eternal. Immortality consumes me—and me only.

The Reverend's Christmas card is born from fire. In the Doctor's grate.

On the corner of Eighth Street and Sixth Avenue, every morning, there is a circular pool of mulch, like a vast bread pizza, like a physical calamity awaiting clearance by some twelve-foot drunk or mutant dog sickened by its own size. No. An old lady descends from the black branches of the fire escape every morning and wearily gathers it all up and clambers home with it in paper bags: the food left for her by the birds.

Every Monday morning, in Dr. Hotchkiss's rooms on the ninth floor, we have Mortality Conference. Diseased organs are passed from doctor to doctor on plastic lunch trays.

*   *   *

John has become more appreciative of Irene. After several desultory attempts, followed by a brief (and nurse-crammed) estrangement and then one big fight, he has reestablished their relationship on a sexual footing. I find I am not as pleased by this as I thought I might be. Jealousy is a new one on me, and amply terrible.

Are we to jump to the unlikely conclusion that John's heart has at last been melted by the love of a good woman? A fat woman, too, of a certain age, one who forgives everything and looks over us when we sleep—who is, let's face it, more like a mother than a lover? The turning point or empowering moment came with the telling of Irene's "secret." Her words themselves broke a long silence.

"She was a girl," said Irene. "She's with foster parents now. In Pennsylvania. I couldn't look after her. I was suicidal."

John snorted and said, "That makes two of us."

"There's something I never told you. I had a child."

They were in bed together at the time, staring sadly at the ceiling. Then one thing led to another.

It's paradoxical, because John doesn't like women who have children. They can have husbands. They can have as many boyfriends as they want. But no kids. When he accidentally gets talking to women who have children, it's practically the first question he asks them—it's the first test they face. And then nothing ever comes of it. Lots of nurses, plenty of sisters. Many matrons. But no mothers.

All three of us know that John has a secret. Only one of us knows what that secret is. He leaves it undisclosed, which is perhaps the best thing to do with secrets.

For most of our lives we are all doctors to ourselves. Not when we're old, and everything feels so numb and dead, and decency and disgust forbid inquiry. And not when we are young, and the body is an unexamined ecstasy. Just the time in between. Mark them, in coffee shops, on buses, wincing, wondering, doctors to themselves, medicine men and faith healers, diagnosticians and anesthetists, silent consultants to themselves.

Doctor yourself. But don't doctor others. Leave them alone. Let them be.

If John's moral life came to me I would say:

There is malocclusion and diplopia. The pulse is thready. Auscultation would reveal dyspnea, rich in rales, also tachypnea, suggesting mediastinal crunch. Eyes show strabismus and nystagmus, also arteriovenous nicking and silver-wiring. In the mouth the buccal mucosae are lesioned, the oropharynx inflamed. The heart: thrills, lifts, heaves, rubs, with a systolic ejection murmur at both sternal borders. Mental status: alert, oriented; memory, judgment, mood—normal.

Meanwhile, on their beds and trolleys, the victims look on with anxious facies.

You can see the stars, now, in the city, or everybody else can, and not just an attractive smattering here and there. No: the inordinate cosmos. Most people behave as if the stars have been visible all along. To them it's no big deal. But John likes the stars, surprisingly. His eyes roam the heavens, the patterns, the clusters. He will pick out these celebrated nightspots to the cooing nurse on his arm, and meticulously expatiate, say, on their relative distances to the earth—and to each other. It's interesting. Those two there that look like twins half an inch apart: they may in fact be nauseatingly sundered by a long light-time of depth, united only by the angle of our point of view. One a dwarf, one a giant . . . The nurses smile and half-listen, their thoughts hardly less fantastic, but much more local. Me, I'm all ears. For to me the stars are motelike, just twists of dust. Yet I feel their fire. How they burn my sight.

Some affairs actually now begin with a medical procedure. John has started bringing his work home. There's nowhere to hide. There's nowhere to hang in the dark.

These prospective lady friends arrive quietly. John, who is ready, receives them quietly. They feel cold, and rest and cry for a while, and then mount the cleared table. They assume their half of the missionary position, though John, of course, is busy elsewhere, with the full steel bowl. A rectangular placenta and a baby about half an inch long with a heart but no face are implanted with the aid of forceps and speculum. He is always telling the women to be quiet. They *must* be quiet. The full bowl bleeds. Next, the digital examination and the swab. They can get down now, and drink something, and talk in whispers. They say goodbye. He'll be seeing them. In about eight weeks, on average.

I am tentatively concluding that these are the bomb babies of Tod Friendly's dreams. It adds up. The babies, so to speak, are helplessly powerful. This is the power they wield: the mortal importance of no one knowing they are there. Naturally, there are asymmetries: in the waking reality it is the mother who must be silent, not the baby. And these babies are incapable of sound: they have hearts but no faces, no throats, no mouths to cry. But dreams are like that, aren't they. Dreams enjoy their own obliquity. After all, John Young, who daily straddles a storm of souls, which kick up in the wind like leaves, John Young wears his white coat—but no black boots. He wears gym shoes, or regular loafers, or of course those wooden clogs of his.

Nearby, the siren of an ambulance cries like a mad

baby, its pitch rising as it passes us and heads on down the street.

Put simply, the hospital is an atrocity-producing situation. Atrocity will follow atrocity, unstoppably. As if fresh atrocity were necessary to validate the atrocity that came before. As if the atrocity that came before was necessary to validate the atrocity that will come after. Stop now and . . . But you can't stop.

Atrocity upon atrocity, and then more atrocity, and then more.

I'm glad it's not my body that is actually touching their bodies. I'm glad I have *his* body, in between. But how I wish I had a body of my own, one that did my bidding. I wish I had a body, just an instrument to feel weary with or through, shoulders that slump, a head that tips back to face the sun, feet that drag, a voice that groans or sighs or asks hoarsely for forgiveness.

I don't understand. Irene still comes to the apartment but we never see her anymore except by accident. It's over. She seems cheerful: she seems relieved. Twice a week she vengefully looks in here to dust the place, and dirty all the dishes, and worry the bed. She leaves like four bucks on the kitchen counter—though it's since gone down to three fifty.

I don't understand. At the hospital we reward our victims with money. I pay the hospital. Irene pays me. I don't get it. Are we all slaves? Are we somehow less than slaves?

They wouldn't believe me, even if I could tell them. They would turn away, in excruciation and contempt.

I'm like the baby taken from the toilet. I have a heart but I don't have a face: I don't have any eyes to cry. Nobody knows I'm here.

Is it a war we are fighting, a war against health, against life and love? My condition is a torn condition. Every day, the dispensing of existence. I see the face of suffering. Its face is fierce and distant and ancient.

There's probably a straightforward explanation for the impossible weariness I feel. A perfectly straightforward explanation. It is a mortal weariness. Maybe I'm tired of being human, if human is what I am. I'm tired of being human.

Part II

4

You do what you do best, not what's best to do

We set sail for Europe in the summer of 1948—for Europe, and for war. Well, I say *we*, but by now John Young was pretty much on his own out there.

Some sort of bifurcation had occurred, in about 1959, or maybe even earlier. I was still living inside, quietly, with my own thoughts. Thoughts that were free to wander through time.

Our ship is loud with all the tongues of Europe, under the big sky and its zoo of cumulus—its snow leopards and polar bears. On the lower deck, where all the people are, there is the sense of an outrageous and clarifying happiness. When it is happy, the human face seeks a particular angle: perhaps you could pinpoint it—thirteen degrees, say, from the horizontal. Also, happiness contains its own ferocity: the right to life and love, fiercely seized. John Young is always especially smart and handsome when he visits the lower deck for his strolls, morning and evening, with ivory-topped cane, with burnished black shoes, with plausible perfecto. Rather forbiddingly he saunters along the lower rink, past the clumps of families, the young mothers, the babies' cries. The cries of babies: we all know what *they* mean, in any language. Everybody seems to have at least one baby, suddenly. As if to get them safely stowed, before the violent renewal of war.

To begin with, the voyage seemed a form of evasive action, a form of flight. The sea glared on with a million eyes, a million witnesses to our getaway. Apart from wanting the law or whatever to catch up with him (which it didn't), I had taken little notice, and no interest, in John's furtive and elaborate preparations for travel—the series of interviews with the Reverend Kreditor, for example. I didn't really wake up until we made the short boat trip to Ellis Island. Of course, months earlier, I had dully taken on the likelihood of major upheaval, on account of what was happening to John's skin. At first it assumed a sallow glow; then, during the cold spring, it went all the way from hot-dog mustard to peanut butter. Jesus, I thought. Jaundice. Then

I twigged: it was a suntan. I put two and two together. People often get this way before taking stylish vacations in exotic locales. The idea of John getting sick, the idea of John coming down with something: that's a good one. His vigor, nowadays, contains something savage and tasteless. It is pink tongued. It is feral—undoctored. The whites of his eyes sting like fresh frost. John's torso now closely resembles one of his more miraculous erections. At any moment and with no warning he'll throw himself onto the floor and do like a hundred push-ups. "Ninety-nine," you'll hear him grunting, ever the literalist. "Ninety-eight. Ninety-seven. Ninety-six." Even during mealtimes, at the captain's table, he's forever girding his muscle and sinew. Under the table his feet jig on their soles. John's body shudders deeper than the ship itself. This war will start at an appointed time, like a ball game. He is thirty-one.

We have our own cabin, scene of many a knee bend and chest flex, on A Deck. There are also communal exercises, on B Deck, which John leads in association with a swarthy purser called Togliatti. We do jumping jacks, and chuck a bit of hooped rope about. To begin with, in the evenings and mornings, during stroll time (the suit, the stick), all the people tended to gather at the sharp end of the ship, looking at where they came from, as people do. Only John is invariably to be found on the stern, looking at where we're headed. The ship's route is clearly delineated on the surface of the water and is violently consumed by our advance. Thus we leave no mark on the ocean, as if we are successfully covering our tracks.

And we seem to have got away with it, likewise. John's feeling tone is buoyant: he seems wonderfully relieved. But if you had me on the table or on the trolley in intensive care—the submarine blip of the oscilloscope (like a lost code), the richly sighing respirator—then I'd be going, going, tumbling end over end. I didn't get away with it. I came too close, I spent too long with suffering and its foul chemical breath; its face is fierce, distant, ancient. The hospital, tepidly humming—I can remember it *all*. To remember a day would take a day. To remember a year would take a year.

Something ails the ship's engines. How they cough and choke and retch. The smoke that feeds our funnels is much too thick and black. Our Greek captain puts in a courtesy visit during dinner and apologizes in his ridiculous English. Often, for days on end, we can only wallow helplessly or make grand clockwise circles. Ugly sea gulls backpedal in our path, seeming to break their fall through the sky. John fumes, like the ship, but the people don't seem to mind. And I quite like it, the sense of suspension, far from land and the means of doing harm. At night, while John's impatient body sleeps, I listen to the waves loosely slapping at the side of the stilled ship.

The slapping sea sounds nice but it's insincere, flattering to deceive, flattering to deceive.

What with John's new fitness program, and the salutary Atlantic air and everything, I myself expected some kind of halfhearted renewal. It didn't really happen. Still, I couldn't help responding, at least in spirit, to the orgy of general joy as we docked at Lisbon; and even John stiffly lent himself to various aromatic embraces. But then the ship idled there for hours, in its own sea mist of impatience and anxiety. Limply I gazed at the mortal oiliness of the water, in which no creature could prosper, and the dockside crowds of welcome floating and swimming above like tropical fish. After that, will and vividness again absented themselves. In fact I tuned out altogether for at least a week, while John checked into the hotel and ran around town shuffling papers and permits and palm grease and all the other shit you deal in when you're firming up a fresh identity. We came out the other side of it with a temporary chauffeur, a good profit, and a really first-rate new name: that of Hamilton de Souza. I am assuming that this identity business is a foible of John's, of Tod's, of Hamilton's, and not universal. But look outside, at the street-skinned hills, the wildernesses of the parks behind their railings, and all the people. This crowd must churn with pseudonyms, with noms de guerre. Those that the war will soon reel in. We've been through three names already. We seem to be able to handle it. Some people, though—you can see it in their faces—some people have no names at all.

Hamilton and I are well established now, of course, in our agreeable villa, with our three maids, plus Tolo the gardener, and the dog, Bustos. It lies in a shallow valley a couple of clicks north of Redondo. Listen: there go the goats, the faint arrhythmia of the bells on their collars, led by the white-clad peasant. The goats are white too, a little herd of souls. The herdsman's infrequent cries are full of the Portuguese melancholy, the Portuguese humanity. Twice a month the fat lawyer whom I think of as the Agent comes to visit in his sweaty suit. We drink white port up on the roof here and converse in formal and limited English. The birds are excited by our garden and by the flowers that shine around us in their troughs and pots.

"So delightful," says the Agent.

"We call that one Bouncing Bet," says Hamilton.

"Charming."

Hamilton points with a finger. "Brown-Eyed Susan."

"So attractive."

"John-Go-To-Bed-At-Noon."

Below, from the lawn, a muscular blackbird crashes into the air.

Around us in the middle distance, which is as near or far as anywhere else seems to get, lie other havens of plaster and flora. I like it here. The villas loom pink and yellow on the arid land, like sweetshops on the planet Mars. The light has the color of fake gold.

We have three servants, Ana and Lourdes, and Rosa, the gypsy girl, to whom I will be obliged to return. I'm familiar with the servant thing, because I had one before: Irene. Oh, Irene! . . . The thing with servants is, you're always cleaning up after them, but not very intensively, it's true, and they're terribly polite. Servants are poor, and I'm talking broke—I mean busted. They give what money they have to the Agent; yet they're always finding that little bit extra, to give to me. Rosa, the girl, is especially insistent. We accept these dues with a seigneurial twinkle. Nobody said it was fair, but at least it's intelligible. What's the trick with money? Money, which might as *well* grow on trees? It all comes down to the quality of your trash. In New York government did it. Here we do our own. Tolo the gardener, with Bustos the dog tensely balanced beside him, on the cart pushed by the mule: they go to the village dump. Or we rely on fire. Quality not quantity. Our trash is *class* trash. Rosa, who is poorest of all, lives in the gypsy camp over the slope at the far end of the valley. We sometimes stroll out that way, in the evenings, and wait, and then discreetly precede her when she walks to the villa; she never turns, but she knows we're there. The camp is made of trash but none of it is any good. Trash. I am its lord. She its bond-maid or prisoner.

Our hobbies?

Well, strolling. Impeccably turned out in twills and tweed, with hunting cap, with Bustos bouncing at our feet. It's an appealing notion, that animals should contain the souls of gods. You can believe it of a cat. Even a mule. You can't believe it of Bustos, loose-skinned and entirely frivolous, with his entreating eyes. The hide-faced peasants, the burdened women clad in black, they croak a furtive greeting, which Hamilton de Souza spiritedly returns. He picked up the lingo right away, but I can't get any kind of fix on it. The only word I feel at home with is *somos*. There's a game we play, Bustos and I, with that saliva-steeped tennis ball of his; and he likes to twirl those sticks. Across the valley, to the slope. The camp really is very dirty.

Oh, and gardening, too. No hands-on stuff, like at Wellport. We stand over Tolo's bent form, and point with our cane. The flowers are amusing, but dreadfully vulgar. All those bursts of pink and crimson.

Our other hobby is gold. We collect it. We amass it. About once a month, with the Agent, we motor to Lisbon and pay a call on an elderly Spaniard in his office at the Hotel de Luxe. We have money ready, supplied by the Agent. We count the florid bank notes and hand them over across the desk. Then, after the old guy has examined, weighed, and wrapped it in a turquoise napkin, we get our gold, in little ingots the size of collar studs. Lassitude and shame and a dreamy disgust provide the medium for these transactions. We sit there, leaden. The heavy brown furniture, and Señor Menini: his eyepiece, the solder in his teeth, his dusty scales. Hamilton and I grow rich in gold.

Can you call Rosa a hobby? Does she qualify? A glimpse of Rosa, as she walks to the well in her pink tatters, and Hamilton's blood slows and clogs, and his hair hums. He just seemed to walk right into that one: love at first sight.

The very day we got here he cornered her in the scullery and embraced her with tears in his eyes, saying *adorada*, *adorada*. Rosa is pink and dirty; she is dusky, she is rosy. One of her duties is to replenish Hamilton's chamber pot each morning. He is usually to be found in his pajama bottoms, shaving, when she comes through the door. In slow declaration he turns toward her. She crouches to place the embarrassingly heavy bowl beneath the bed. She leaves with her eyes on the floor, saying *bom dia*. Frankly, he's missed the boat with Rosa. She's much too young for Hamilton— or for anybody else, probably, except her brothers and her dad and her uncles and so on, or so Hamilton speculates (I can tell), when he skirts the camp at dusk. Last week she celebrated her thirteenth birthday, so now she's only twelve. He watches her in the yard with her cloth and bucket, as she kneels to tackle the clean plates. The slope of her back, the way she wipes her brow. In her luminous scraps of clothes she is pink and bruised, like the inside of her mouth, the teeth still both big and little. Soon, to fill those gaps, she will get some milk teeth, purchased from the tooth fairy. . . . In women, what is he looking for, mother, daughter, sister, wife? Where *is* his wife? She'd better turn up soon, while there's still time. Rosa gives him presents, which, on his trips to Lisbon, Hamilton fondly redeems.

But the body he is most interested in, these days, is his own. He is his own hobby. And his body is its own lover. What a love is this, between upper limb and external heart. Christ no, it's not like the Wellport days, back when: poor old Tod and his one-man no-shows, his lone fiascos. Hamilton just can't get over it, his body. You would think he'd never had one before. As he moves through the house, mirrors monitor him. Him, it, this, this: *this* is the body he primes and mortifies and shrewdly inspects in all the rippling fun-house mirrors of Portugal.

There are poems to Rosa, which he takes from the trash. They are brought in the wicker wastepaper basket by bowing Lourdes. Never more than two or three lines long.

> The soul of a princess in her gypsy rags,
> Doomed to fret in her humble stall . . .

And:

> Rosa, whose innocence asks to be saved!
> Where the knight who will deliver her?

Yeah. Where the knight. These lines of his he moodily and sometimes tearfully erases with his pen—a good image, perhaps, of his chronic diffidence.

His body now exudes this pink gook which he subsequently bottles and gives to the Agent together with a bunch of other toiletries.

When he goes out there to wait for her in the evening, I sometimes think: It isn't Rosa. It's the camp he loves. The fierce and sentimental music and the ignorant colors, the prettiness and the disease under the fake-gold light, the tuberculosis and syphilis, the fires showing through the branches like illuminated brains, the glamorous nomas of eye and mouth, the childishness and all the valueless trash. He wants to do something to the camp. What? Here in Portugal he pretends not to be a doctor, probably wisely, and steers well clear of anyone who is sick or injured, Lourdes with her dramatic fevers or Tolo knock-kneed with gout, even Rosa's scrapes and sprains. He leaves it to the local man: the local man, whose tremulous reliance on a few patented drugs Hamilton observes with a speechless sneer. But he wants to do something to the camp. He wants to doctor it.

Mind and body are preparing for war. The body, during the waking hours, with its regimes, its saturnalias of self. The mind at night. Something is savaging his sleep. Surprised into consciousness, alone in the black hemisphere, he cries until he laughs; then he uses the chamber pot that Rosa readied, and goes back to sleep quickly, despite the pain. Somewhere in the severe dance of this roiling sleep I can sense the beginnings of a profound rearrangement, as if everything bad might soon be good, as if everything wrong might soon be right. Admittedly this new recurring dream of his, in bald summary, doesn't sound particularly encouraging, but I think it's ambivalent and could go either way. He dreams he is shitting human bones. . . . Now and then, when the night sky is starless, I look up and form the hilarious suspicion that the world will soon start making sense.

One hot afternoon I came down from my bedroom, after a brief but taxing siesta, to see the Agent pull up in his outlandish Packard. Over a cognac he gloomily informs us of the Japanese surrender. Lourdes and Ana, I notice, have tears in their eyes and keep crossing themselves. The Agent tells me apologetically about the superstitious fears of these simple people. The end of the world. *A bomba atómica* . . . I was astonished. So! They did it. They had to go ahead and do it. Just when world abolition looked like a certainty. They couldn't resist: limited nuclear war. . . . Rather rudely, perhaps, Hamilton decided to take Bustos for a romp and leave them all to it. On our return the Agent had gone and the women were calm, unlike Bustos, that foolish puppy, who spins at my feet and fixes me with his heartbroken eyes.

There is a growing coldness in the household. Emotion is retreating from it. This is how things should be. Rosa, who

still works for us, has safely escaped into childhood. The
gaze that Hamilton turns toward her no longer moves softly
across her face, her pink rags. This is fit. We will now be
able to take our leave of Rosa with a quick nod, a little
inclination from the vertical. I won't even miss Bustos,
which the Agent dragged off months ago.

War wasn't going to come to us. War wasn't going to roll
through *our* village. We were going to be inserted into it—
with what they call surgical precision. With slow care.

One was not sorry to bid farewell to Portugal and its
rhythm of misery and fiesta, the docks, the Agent's clueless
stare. And one did what one could with the conditions on
the sordid steamer. Actually Hamilton himself, so smart and
handsome when he travels, soon looked as grimy and fatalistic as everybody else. There were about twenty passengers
(this was no passenger ship) and we slept in the mess, on
benches and deck chairs, much resented by the crew, each
of us with his possessions, or his secret, crushed like a lover
in his arms and whispered to in all the languages of
Europe. . . . The other language, stoppered in Hamilton's
throat: it is climbing to the surface. It twitches inside
him. . . . Of course, we converse with no man: just sighs
and nods and frowns, speech-waivers. They play cards all
day. They are low persons, flotsam. What does the war want
of them? They look fully disgraced. We have our gold,
stored in a second belt beneath our shirt, and tugging heavily
on our nethers.

I had always thought of Italy as my spiritual home.
Hence the initial disappointment of Salerno. We stayed in a
cheap boardinghouse from which the landlord saw fit to evict
us for all the hours of daylight; strolling abroad, we devoted
our time to churchgoing and to incoherent altercations with

the Italian police. Hamilton, it turns out, despite his observances of the Wellport era, has no great liking for churches.
He sits in the first pew he comes to and leers at the door
every twenty seconds with the frowsiest of sighs. Once he
approached the altar and extinguished a candle on the chest
there, and pocketed a few imperceptible coins. A single
glance at the crucified Christ, the worshiped corpse: a figure
bent like a branch whose shape has changed in the stretching
agony of fire. Above our head, an unregarded observatory
of light. Then out again to the open air and the waiting
carbinieri and the dumb show of *pappaciere* and *papieri*.

A vaudevillian menace charged our journey to Rome,
the locomotive black and chimerical, and the Stazione Ter-
mini like an anti-cathedral with its soot-stained glass and
vaultlike coldness and smell of earth's crust or hell's rafters.
Boldly we made our way through the incredible promiscuity
of the streets: men with shoes made out of silver-birch bark,
women wearing sacks and carpets, children in their dusty
birthday suits. Their faces: they look like people on their
way into hospital, as if life is worryingly but fascinatingly
strange. Such unanimity of stun and daze. It's okay, I want
to tell them. We're all going to make it. None will vanish.
Many will appear. A cordial welcome—and a light lunch—
awaited us at the monastery (Franciscan) on the Via Sicilia.
After that we were off out again. Where to? Where else.
The Vatican.

We become quite a regular there, as a matter of fact,
nine consecutive mornings, including two Sundays, past the
battlements, through gardens, then down the long loot-
crammed passages, with glass cases full of baubles and beauties, and oblongs of oils and tapestries and embroidered maps
reeling past our sight—to the waiting room. Actually Father
Duryea, our contact, our man, always saw us right away;

but that didn't stop Hamilton from hanging around for hours afterward, in the waiting room. Tense, silent, on the chair by the table with its flower bowl and its dish of cracked apples. Father Duryea was an Irishman. His rampant facial heat had set up its headquarters in his nose; from there, stray tendrils of blood seemed to leak into his remorseful gray eyes. His mouth, too, was a scene of pain. His poor mouth. Hamilton greeted him with emotional thanks and immediately surrendered our papers: our little Nansen passport, our Portuguese visa, even the ticket coupon with which we had been issued at the harbor of Salerno. Father Duryea appeared to be hopeful and indulgent. But these things take time. Time in the waiting room, staring at the wounded apples and their open flesh.

Time in the monastery on the Via Sicilia—where Hamilton seems to have taken his own vow of silence. The food I fill the plate with there reflects the character of the institution: it is simple, but perfectly sustaining. We have our own little cell. The monastery is full of wayfarers like me, ghosts with half a name (I feel I'm *between* names at the moment). The Vatican is full of supplicants like me, calling, "Father. Father." Europe, probably, is full of people like me, adjusting our stance for the lurch into war. So I am lonely, but not alone, like everybody else. Shame heats our cell, and push-ups, and prayers. Yes, prayers. His prayers are like the noise you make to drown out an insupportable thought. I might be impressed and affected by this sudden talent for suffering, if it weren't for its monotony: fear, just fear, fear only. Why? We're all going to make it. Yet with hands clasped he whimpers and gibbers with such desperate ardor for his own preservation, on his knees. To show good faith, or to show something, he even tried a thing with . . . you know: the chair, the belt suspended from the rafter. It didn't work, needless to say. As I took the trouble to explain earlier, you can't do that. You can't do that, not once you're here.

Yesterday we found a photograph, under the bushes behind the willow trees. In small scraps—we pieced it together. The face of a young woman: dark, downy, pleasant, direct. Not especially forgiving. I fear that's our wife.

How heavy it is to sit there in the waiting room, on the chair, by the table, with one's penitent perfecto, watching the cankered apples heal.

"We help those that need," said Father Duryea, on our final visit, "not those that deserve."

"You do what you do best," said Hamilton, "not what's best to do."

"I'll do what I can."

"I can't explain what I did. I can't ask you to help me."

"Ah now."

"I'm nothing. I'm dead. I'm just . . . I'm not even . . ."

Father Duryea sat up. And so did I. In a deep and distant voice Hamilton went on, "I lost my idea of the gentleness of human flesh."

"Explain," said Father Duryea.

"We lost our feeling about the human body. Children even. Tiny babies."

So. Sense. Here it comes. It's all coming out. It's been in here too long and now it's all coming out. The corridors and theaters, the Peter Pan Ward, the desk-top terminations, the eyes of the unlistened-to: that world of pain with darkness at the bottom of it.

Father Duryea's face contracted around the scorched core of his nose. And he said, "I understand."

"You know where I was. In a situation like that certain acts suggested themselves."

"I understand, my son."

"The situation was mad and impossible."

"There is no need to say."

Hamilton moistened his cheeks with his sleeve and sniffed richly. "There were things . . ."

"Speak."

"I still want to heal, Father. Perhaps, that way, by doing good . . ."

"Hell?"

"I've been to hell."

"Of course. Of course."

"I have sinned, Father."

"You seem troubled, my child."

At this point Hamilton handed over our various *laissez-passer*, and Father Duryea presented him with his new documents. Before doing so, Father Duryea stared at them for many arduous minutes. Stared at them with his bleeding eyes. Our parting was marked by the usual formalities, the usual compliments paid to my unimprovable English.

Hamilton and I spent our last night in Rome at a very respectable hotel on the Via Garibaldi, near the high walls of the prison. So high were these prison walls, indeed, that they left you wondering at the build of the common Italian criminal. I pictured a menagerie of depraved and black-toothed giraffes, each with his slashback and switchblade. . . . We even had our own bathroom, in whose tub we wallowed for well over an hour. Clean breast. Clean hands.

Our name has changed once more. I don't think it will ever change again. Rather alarmingly at first, it has to be said, we are now called Odilo Unverdorben.

And clean heels. Our journey north was *charmed*. We were the baton in a relay race to war.

111

By train to Bologna (where I bought my hiking boots), by truck to Rovereto; thenceforward we moved in daily spurts of twenty or twenty-five miles, always accompanied or monitored, from village to village, farm to farm, on foot, by cart, in preposterous automobiles. And the land shown me by my guides, my deliverers, how painterly it was, the buildings of earthen crockery, the stone variegated like pork brawn in the mild breath of dusk. How thickly grassed and trimly forested: here, and now, the earth has good hair, thick and trim, and a good scalp beneath, not like *there*, not like *before*, all patched and pocked. The land is innocent. It never did anything.

March and February we spent on the Brenner, where we lodged at three different farmsteads. While hardly ideal, our living arrangements were suitably ascetic, and conducive to inner preparation. Personally I longed for human society and for exercise (a good long tramp, for example), but no doubt Odilo had his reasons. Had his reasons for those weeks spent in hayloft and cowshed under a mound of blankets with nothing to do but pray and shiver. We heard the distinct whispers of dawn and dusk, and the dogs barking, but no further rumor of war. It was snowing on the day we resumed our northward journey. Snowing patiently, for there was much of it on the ground, many snowflakes to be restored like white souls to the heavens. By jeep and truck we moved swiftly up through the towns and cities of middle Europe. Much of it was junk and trash, awaiting collection by war. Buildings were black, awaiting the color of fire. People were smudged, trampled, awaiting the hooves and treads of armies. Europe churned in the night like the seas of human forms round the stoves of station waiting rooms. Everywhere I went, their expressions charged with power and delight, men gave me gold.

I knew all this gold was sacred and indispensable to our mission. Accordingly, at the final staging post, the final farm, within view of the River Vistula, where we lived well and warmly, and there were the heads of children to pat and tousle, and the striped mattress before the fire—we buried our gold. Swearing most eloquently and solemnly, we buried the pouched filings under a compost heap behind the barn. Of course, the act was merely symbolic: the gold's temporary return to the earth. Because we dug it up again five days later, after the compost heap had gone. When he swears, Odilo invokes human ordure, from which, as we now know, all human good eventually emanates.

How many times have I asked myself: when is the world going to start making sense? Yet the answer is out there. It is rushing toward me over the uneven ground.

Here there is no why

The world is going to start making

sense . . .

. . . Now.

I, Odilo Unverdorben, arrived in Auschwitz Central somewhat precipitately and by motorbike, with a wide twirl or frill of slush and mud, shortly after the Bolsheviks had entrained their ignoble withdrawal. *Now.* Was there a secret passenger on the backseat of the bike, or in some imaginary sidecar? No. I was one. I was also in full uniform. Beyond the southern boundary of the Lager, in a roofless barn, I had slipped out of our coarse traveling clothes and emotionally donned the black boots, the white coat, the fleece-lined jacket, the peaked cap, the pistol. The motorbike I found earlier, wedged into a ditch. Oh how I soared out of there, with what vaulting eagerness, what daring. . . . Now I straddled this heavy machine and revved with jerked gauntlet. Auschwitz lay around me, miles and miles of it, like a somersaulted Vatican. Human life was all ripped and torn. But I was one now, fused for a preternatural purpose.

Your shoulder blades still jolted to the artillery of the Russians as they scurried eastward. What had they done here? Done something as an animal does: just finds it's gone ahead and done it. I reacted on impulse. To tell the truth, I was in less than perfect control of myself. I started shouting (they sounded like shouts of pain and rage). And at whom? At these coat hangers and violin bows, at these aitches and queries and crawling double-U's, ranked like tabloid expletives? I marched; I marched, shouting, over the bridge and across all the railway tracks and into the birch wood—into the place I would come to know as Birkenau. After a short and furious rest in the potato store I entered the women's hospital, inflexibly determined on an inspection. It was not appropriate. I see that now (it was a swoon of where-to-begin?). My arrival only deepened the stupefaction of the few orderlies, never mind the patients, sprawled two or three to a straw sack and still well short of the size of a woman. And rats as big as cats! I was astonished by the power with

116

which my German crashed out of me, as if in millennial anger at having been silenced for so long. In the washroom another deracinating spectacle: marks and pfennigs—good tender—stuck to the wall with human ordure. A mistake: a mistake. What is the *meaning* of this? Ordure, ordure everywhere. Even on my return through the ward, past ulcer and edema, past sleepwalker and sleeptalker, I could feel the hungry suck of it on the soles of my black boots. Outside: everywhere. This stuff, this human stuff, at normal times (and in civilized locales) tastefully confined to the tubes and runnels, subterranean, unseen—this stuff had burst its banks, surging outward and upward onto the floor, the walls, the very ceiling of life. Naturally, I didn't immediately see the logic and justice of it. I didn't immediately see this: that now human shit is out in the open, we'll get a chance to find out what this stuff can really do.

That first morning I was served a rudimentary breakfast in the Officers' Home. I felt quite calm, though I could neither eat nor drink. With my ham and my cheese, which were not of my making, they brought me iced seltzer. There was only one other officer present. I was keen to exercise my German, but we didn't speak. He held his coffee cup as a woman does, with both palms curled around it, for the warmth; and you could hear the china tapping its morse against his teeth. On several occasions he stood up with some serenity and went to the bathroom, and dived back in again gracelessly scrabbling at his belt. This, I soon saw, was a kind of acclimatization. For the first few weeks I was seldom off the toilet bowl myself.

My utterly silent cubicle has a shallow orange bath mat on the floor beside the bed. To welcome the faint dampness of my German feet, as I turn in. To welcome the faint dampness of my German feet, as I rise.

*   *   *

117

During week two the camp started filling up. In dribs and drabs, at first, then in flocks and herds. All this I watched through a spyhole, under a workbench in a disused supply hut toward the birch wood, with blanket, kümmel bottle—and rosary, fingered like an abacus, as I counted them in. I realized I had seen a few of these same processions on my way north through eastern Czechoslovakia, in Zilina and in Ostrava. The hearty trek and the bracing temperatures had obviously done the men good, though their condition, on arrival, still left much to be desired. And *there weren't enough of them.* As in a dream one was harrowed by questions of scale, by impenetrable disparities. In their hundreds, even in their thousands, these stragglers could never fill the gaping universe of the Kat-Zet. Another source, another power-house, was desperately needed. . . . The short days were half over by the time I ventured from the hut (where my motorbike was also preserved. I kept examining it in a fond fever). The officers' clubroom was busier now, and there were always new arrivals. It felt strange—no, it felt right that we should all know each other, as it were automatically: we, who had gathered here for a preternatural purpose. My German worked like a dream, like a brilliant robot you switch on and stand back and admire as it does all the hard work. Courage was arriving too, in uniformed human units, the numbers and the special daring adequate to the task we faced. How handsome men are. I mean their shoulders, their tremendous necks. By the end of the second week our club-house was the scene of strident song and bold laughter. One night, bumping into the doorway, and stepping over a colleague, I made my way out into the sleet, the toilets all being occupied, and as I crouched, steadying my cheek against the cold planks, I peered through the reeking shadows of Auschwitz and saw that the nearest ruins were fuming more

118

than ever and had even begun to glow. There was a new smell in the air. The sweet smell.

We needed magic, to resolve significance from what surrounded us, which scarcely permitted contemplation: we needed someone godlike—someone who could turn this world around. And in due course he came. . . . Not a tall man, but of the usual dimensions; coldly beautiful, true, with self-delighted eyes; graceful, chasteningly graceful in his athletic authority; and a doctor. Yes, a simple doctor. It was quite an entrance, I don't mind telling you. Flashing through the birch wood came the white Mercedes-Benz, from which he leapt in his greatcoat and then dashed across the yard yelling out orders. I knew his name, and murmured it as I looked on from the supply hut, with my schnapps and my toilet paper: "Uncle Pepi." The trash and wreckage before him was now shivering with fire as he stood, hands on hips, watching all his powers gather in the smoke. I turned slowly away and felt the rush and zip of violently animated matter. When, with a shout, I jerked my eye back to its hole, there was no smoke anywhere, only the necessary building, perfect, even to the irises and the low picket fence that lined its path, before which "Uncle Pepi" now stood, with one arm crooked and raised. Even to the large sign above the door: BRAUSEBAD. "Sprinkleroom," I whispered, with a reverent snort. But now "Uncle Pepi" moved on. That morning, as I lay on the wooden floor of the supply hut with my teeth chattering in anticipation, I heard five more explosions. Velocity and fusion sucking up the shocked air. By the next day we were ready to go to work.

What tells me that this is right? What tells me that all the rest was wrong? Certainly not my aesthetic sense. I would never claim that Auschwitz-Birkenau-Monowitz was good to look at. Or to listen to, or to smell, or to taste, or to touch. There was, among my colleagues there, a general though desultory quest for greater elegance. I can understand that word, and all its yearning: *elegant*. Not for its elegance did I come to love the evening sky above the Vistula, hellish red with the gathering souls. Creation is easy. Also ugly. *Hier ist kein warum.* Here there is no why. Here there is no when, no how, no where. Our preternatural purpose? To dream a race. To make a people from the weather. From thunder and from lightning. With gas, with electricity, with shit, with fire.

I or a doctor of equivalent rank was present at every stage in the sequence. One did not need to know why the ovens were so ugly, so very ugly. A tragically burly insect eight feet tall and made out of rust. Who would want to cook with an oven such as this? Pulleys, plungers, grates, and vents were the organs of the machine. . . . The patients, still dead, were delivered out on a stretcherlike apparatus. The air felt thick and warped with the magnetic heat of creation. Thence to the Chamber, where the bodies were stacked carefully and, in my view, counterintuitively, with babies and children at the base of the pile, then the women and the elderly, and then the men. It was my stubborn belief that it would be better the other way round, because the little ones surely risked injury under that press of naked weight. But it worked. Sometimes, my face rippling pecu- liarly with smiles and frowns, I would monitor proceedings through the viewing slit. There was usually a long wait while the gas was invisibly introduced by the ventilation grills. The dead look so dead. Dead bodies have their dead body language. It says nothing. I always felt a gorgeous relief at the moment of the first stirring. Then it was ugly again. Well, we cry and twist and are naked at both ends of life.

We cry at both ends of life, while the doctor watches. It was I, Odilo Unverdorben, who personally removed the pellets of Zyklon B and entrusted them to the pharmacist in his white coat. Next, the facade of the Sprinkleroom, the function of whose spouts and nozzles (and numbered seats and wardrobe tickets, and signs in six or seven languages) was merely to reassure and not, alas, to cleanse; and the garden path beyond.

Clothes, spectacles, hair, spinal braces, and so on—these came later. Entirely intelligibly, though, to prevent needless suffering, the dental work was usually completed while the patients were not yet alive. The *Kapos* would go at it, crudely but effectively, with knives or chisels or any tool that came to hand. Most of the gold we used, of course, came direct from the Reichsbank. But every German present, even the humblest, gave willingly of his own store—I more than any other officer save "Uncle Pepi" himself. I *knew* my gold had a sacred efficacy. All those years I amassed it, and polished it with my mind: for the Jews' teeth. The bulk of the clothes were contributed by the Reich Youth Leadership. Hair for the Jews came courtesy of Filzfabrik A.G. of Roth, near Nuremberg. Freight cars full of it. Freight car after freight car.

At this point, notwithstanding, I should like to log one of several possible caveats or reservations. In the Sprinkleroom the patients eventually get dressed in the clothes provided, which, though seldom very clean, are at least always pertinently cut. Here, the guards have a habit of touching the women. Sometimes—certainly—to bestow a jewel, a ring, a small valuable. But at other times quite gratuitously. Oh, I think they mean well enough. It is done in the irrepressible German manner: coltishly, and with lit face. And they only do it to the angry ones. And it definitely has the effect of calming them down. One touch, there, and they go all numb and blocked, like the others. (Who wail sometimes. Who stare at us with incredulous scorn. But I understand their condition. I'm sympathetic; I accept all that.) It may be symbolic, this touching of the women. Life and love must go on. Life and love must emphatically and resonantly go on: here, that's what we're all about. Yet there is a patina of cruelty, intense cruelty, almost as if creation corrupts. . . . I don't want to touch the girls' bodies. As is well known, I frown on such harassment. I don't even want to look at them. The bald girls with their enormous eyes. Just made, and all raw from their genesis. I'm a *little* worried by it: I mean, this fastidiousness is so out of character. The delicacy of the situation, with their parents and often their grandparents there and everything (as in a thwarted erotic dream), would hardly explain the lack of visual stimulation; and I get on like a house on fire with the girls in the officers' bordello. No. I think it must have something to do with my wife.

The overwhelming majority of the women, the children, and the elderly we process with gas and fire. The men, of course, as is right, walk a different path to recovery. *Arbeit Macht Frei* says the sign on the gate, with typically gruff and unde-signing eloquence. The men work for their freedom. There they go now, in the autumn dusk, the male patients in their light pajamas, while the band plays. They march in ranks of five, in their wooden clogs. Look. There's a thing they do, with their heads. They bend their heads right back until their faces are entirely open to the sky. I've tried it. I try to do it, and I can't. There's this fist of flesh at the base of my neck, which the men don't yet have. The men come here awful thin. You can't get a stethoscope to them. The bell bridges on their ribs. Their hearts sound far away.

There they go, to the day's work, with their heads bent back. I was puzzled at first but now I know why they do it, why they stretch their throats like that. They are looking for the souls of their mothers and their fathers, their women and their children, gathering in the heavens—awaiting human form, and union. . . . The sky above the Vistula is full of stars. I can see them now. They no longer hurt my eyes.

These familial unions and arranged marriages, known as *selections on the ramp*, were the regular high points of the KZ routine. It is a commonplace to say that the triumph of Auschwitz was essentially organizational: we found the sacred fire that hides in the human heart—and built an autobahn that went there. But how to explain the divine synchronies of the ramp? At the very moment that the weak and young and old were brought from the Sprinkleroom to the railway station, as good as new, so their menfolk completed the appointed term of labor service and ventured forth to claim them, on the ramp, a trifle disheveled to be sure, but strong and sleek from their regime of hard work and strict diet. As matchmakers, we didn't know the meaning of the word *failure*; on the ramp, stunning successes were as cheap as spit. When the families coalesced, how their hands and eyes would plead for one another, under our indulgent gaze. We toasted them far into the night. One guard, his knees bent and swaying, played an accordion. Actually we all drank like fiends. The stag party on the ramp, and the *Kapos*, like the groom's best friends, shoving the man into the waiting cart—freshly sprayed with trash and shit—for the journey home.

The Auschwitz universe, it has to be allowed, was fiercely coprocentric. It was *made* of shit. In the early months I still had my natural aversion to overcome, before I understood the fundamental strangeness of the process of fruition.

Enlightenment was urged on me the day I saw the old Jew float to the surface of the deep latrine, how he splashed and struggled into life, and was hoisted out by the jubilant guards, his clothes cleansed by the mire. Then they put his beard back on. I also found it salutary to watch the *Scheissekommando* about its work. This team had the job of replenishing the ditches from the soil wagon, not with buckets or anything like that but with flat wooden spades. In fact a great many of the camp's labor programs were quite clearly unproductive. They weren't destructive either. Fill that hole. Dig it up again. Shift that. Then shift it back. Therapy was the order of the day. . . . The *Scheissekommando* was made up of our most cultured patients: academics, rabbis, writers, philosophers. As they worked, they sang arias, and whistled scraps of symphonies, and recited poetry, and talked of Heine, and Schiller, and Goethe . . . In the officers' club, when we are drinking (which we nearly always are), and where shit is constantly mentioned and invoked, we sometimes refer to Auschwitz as Anus Mundi. And I can think of no finer tribute than that.

There are other revealing examples of camp argot. The main Ovenroom is called *Heavenblock*, its main approach road *Heavenstreet*. Chamber and Sprinkleroom are known, most mordantly, as *the central hospital*. *Sommerfrische* is our name for a tour of duty here, in any season: "summer air," suggesting a perennial vacation from an inadequate reality. When we mean *never* we say *tomorrow morning*—it's like the Spanish saying *mañana*. The slenderest patients, those whose faces are nothing more than a triangle of bone around the eyes, they're *Muselmänner:* not, as I first thought, as an ironical glance at *musclemen*. No. The angularity of hip and shoulder suggests *Muslims*—Muslims at prayer. Of course, they're not Muslims. They're Jews. Well, we converted them! When will it happen, the conversion of the Jews? Tomorrow morning. The rumor and gossip, which often tend to overexcite the male patients, we leniently designate as *latrine talk*.

Hier ist kein warum. . . . Disappointingly, my German fails to improve. I speak it, and appear to understand it, and give and take orders in it, but on some level it just isn't sinking in. My German is no more advanced than my Portuguese. I think it took a lot out of me learning colloquial English. That was my shot. It's a funny language, German. For one thing, everybody shouts it. All those very long words: the literalism, the tinkertoy accumulation. It sounds pushy, beginning every sentence with a verb like that. And take the first person singular: *ich*. "*Ich*." Not a masterpiece of reassurance, is it? *I* sounds nobly erect. *Je* has a certain strength and intimacy. *Eo*'s okay. *Yo* I can really relate to. Yo! But *ich*? It's like the sound a child makes when it confronts its own . . . Perhaps that's part of the point. No doubt all will come clear as soon as my German gets better. When will that be? I know. Tomorrow morning!

In the officers' bordello, which is situated, appropriately, at the far corner of the Experimental Block (its windows permanently shuttered or boarded), I have changed the amatory habits of a lifetime. Much of the old thoroughness has gone. Much of the attention to detail that was wont to mark my dealings with the gentler sex. It may be an awareness of my married status (of which my colleagues often jokingly remind me), or a way of squaring all my activities with the ethos of the KZ, or a simple boredom with the female face, but now my thrusts of love—so sudden, so hurried, so helpless, so hopeless—are exclusively directed at the source of universal sustenance and fruition. The bald whores give us no money. We ask no questions. Because here there is no why.

Another Kat-Zet usage, widely current, used in many forms: it sounds like *smistig*, but it would appear to be a conflation of two German substantives, *Schmutzstück* and *Schmuckstück*, "garbage" and "jewel." Ironically, again, *smistig* means "come to an end," "concluded," "finished."

I have started corresponding with my wife, whose name is Herta. Herta's letters come, not from the fire (*das Feuer*), but from the trash (*der Plunder*). And they are in German. My letters to Herta are brought to me by the valet. I laboriously erase them, here, at night, in the silent room. I am left with nice sheets of white paper. But what for? My letters are in German too, though they contain gobbets of English that are playfully pedagogic in tone. I think it makes sense that Herta and I should get to know each other in this way. We're pen pals.

It seems that my wife has already conceived her doubts about the work we are doing here. Obviously the misunderstanding will have to be cleared up. There is also the matter of the baby (*das Baby*). "My darling, my one, my all, there will be other babies," I write, somewhat confusingly. "There will be *lots* of little babies." I don't much like the sound of this. Is the baby—is *das Baby* the *bomb* baby? The baby that has such power over its parents? I don't think so. Our baby (which has a name: Eva) exerts colossal power *as a subject*. But not the physical power that the bomb baby exerted, over its parents and over everybody else in the black room: some thirty souls.

The photograph of her I found in Rome, in the gardens of the monastery—I take it out and look at it. At night my eyes are full of tears. By day I throw myself into my work. I wonder if there will be any end to the sacrifices I am being asked to make.

*   *   *

"Uncle Pepi" was everywhere. This being the thing that was most often said about him. For instance, "It's as if he's everywhere," or "The man seems to be everywhere," or, more simply, " 'Uncle Pepi' is everywhere." Omnipresence was only one of several attributes that tipped him over into the realm of the superhuman. He was also fantastically clean, for Auschwitz; when he was present, and he was present everywhere, I could sense the various cuts and nicks on my queasy jawline, my short but disobedient hair, the unhappy hang of my uniform, my lusterless black boots. His face was feline in shape, wide at the temples, and his blink was as slow as any cat's. On the ramp he cut a frankly glamorous figure, where he moved like a series of elegant decisions. You felt that he was only playing the part of a human being. Self-isolated as he was, "Uncle Pepi" nonetheless displayed the best kind of condescension, and was in fact unusually collegial—not so much with youngsters like myself, of course, but with more senior medical figures, like Thilo and Wirths. I was moreover privileged—and on something like a regular basis—to assist "Uncle Pepi" in Room 1 on Block 20 and later in Block 10 itself.

I recognized Room 1 from my dreams. The pink rubber apron on its hook, the instrument bowls and thermoses, the bloody cotton, the half-pint hypodermic with its foot-long needle. This is the room, I had thought, where something mortal would be miserably decided. But dreams are playful, and love to tease and poke fun at the truth. . . . Already showing signs of life, patients were brought in one by one from the pile next door and wedged onto the chair in Room 1, which looked like what it was, a laboratory in the Hygienic Institute, a world of bubbles and bottles. With the syringe there were two ways to go, intravenous and cardiac,

"Uncle Pepi" tending to champion the latter as more efficient and humane. We did both. Cardiac: the patient blindfolded with a towel, his right hand placed in the mouth to stifle his own whimpers, the needle eased into the dramatic furrow of the fifth rib space. Intravenous: the patient with his forearm on the support table, the rubber tourniquet, the visible vein, the needle, the judicious dab of alcohol. "Uncle Pepi" was then sometimes obliged to bring them to their senses with a few slaps about the face. The corpses were pink and blue-bruised. Death was pink but yellowish, and contained in a glass cylinder labeled *Phenol*. A day of that and you stroll out in your white coat and black boots, with the familiar headache and the plangent perfecto and the breakfast tannic gathering in your throat, and the eastward sky looked like phenol.

He led. We followed. Phenol work became absolutely routine. All of us did it the whole time. It wasn't until later that I saw what "Uncle Pepi" was capable of, in Block 10.

My wife Herta paid her first visit to Auschwitz in the spring of 1944, which was perhaps unfortunate: we were then doing the Hungarian Jews, and at an incredible rate, something like ten thousand a day. Unfortunate, because I was on ramp duty practically every night, finding the work somewhat impersonal too, the *selections* now being made by loudspeaker (such was the weight of traffic), and having little to do but stand there drinking and shouting with my colleagues—thus denying Herta the kind of undivided attention that every young wife craves. . . . Wait. Let me go at this another way.

Everything was ready for her. Thoughtful as ever, Dr. Wirths had made available the annex of his own living quarters— a delightful apartment (with its own kitchen and bathroom) beyond whose patterned lace curtains stood a high white fence. Beyond that, unseen, the benign cacophony of the Kat-Zet . . . Dr. Wirths has his wife and three children with him, at present. I hoped that Herta would spend some of her time playing with the little Wirthses. Though that might touch on a sensitive subject. . . . I was sitting on the sofa, quietly crying; I think I was wishing that Auschwitz looked better than it did, just now, with its windless heat and plagues of flies homing in on the marshes. As I heard the staff car approach I wandered out into the pale brown of the front garden. What did I expect? The familiar awkwardness, I suppose. Reproaches, accusations, sadness—perhaps even feeble blows from feeble fists. All to be at least partly resolved, that first night, in the act of love. Or certainly the second. That's how these things *usually* begin. What I didn't expect was a statement of truth. The truth was the last thing I was ready for. I should have known. The world, after all, here in Auschwitz, has a new habit. It makes sense.

The driver looked on sentimentally as she alighted from the car and made her way down the path. Then she turned to confront me. She looked nothing like her photograph. The girl in the photograph, whose face was clear.

"You are a stranger to me," she said. *Fremder:* stranger.

"Please," I said. "Please. My darling." *Bitte. Liebling.*

"I don't know you," she said. *Ich kenne dich nicht.*

Herta kept her head down as I helped her off with her coat. And something enveloped me, something that was all ready for my measurements, like a suit or a uniform, over and above what I wore, and lined with grief.

Her shyness proved impregnable. We lunched quietly, indeed wordlessly, on the fluidal sausages. Herta was all thumbs with the heavy cutlery and the Swedish glassware. When the servants left, she went and sat on the sofa and stared at the attractive rug. I joined her. She proved immune to my light-headed but rather leaden gallantries, the words so hard to shift around. Actually I felt far from well myself. And worse and worse as the morning wore on. And then entirely terrible, after a convulsive visit to the small but resonant bathroom, whose greasy air was full of racing currents, fire-tinged. I betook myself to bed in some exasperation, and without really bothering to get undressed. When I awoke around four A.M., still in my boots, she was lying beside me, entombed in her woolen nightgown, and fiercely whispering, *Nein. Nie. Nie.* Never. Never. No amount of caresses or endearments (or good-hearted raillery) seemed likely to soften her. I got out of bed—gah!—and then picked myself up off the floor. Herta was now fast asleep. I remember thinking how white and cold and still her face looked, without the breeze of thought or sentience, as I stumbled off to the tumult of the ramp.

Ours was a human enterprise, but the animal kingdom played its part in the new order of being. Cartfuls of corpses were shoved from the burial pits by mules and oxen, and stupidly, with no animal comment. Cows did not look up from their grazing, their indifference seeming to say, *This is all right. This need not be remarked,* as if it wasn't unusual to conjure a multitude from the sky above the river. We kept rabbits, too, in much the same way as we dealt with the people, improvisationally and with desperate brilliance. Men gave up the very linings of their greatcoats to provide the little creatures with fur. And then of course there were the dogs, boxers, their crushed faces, their squat coats bearing the ubiquitous sign of the twisted cross, in honor of the Jews they healed with their teeth and with the snort and quiver of their jaws.

In the clubroom I am told (I think I've got this right): Jews come from monkeys (from *Menschenaffen*), as do Slavs and so on. Germans, on the other hand, have been preserved in ice from the beginning of time in the lost continent of Atlantis. This is good to know. A meteorology division in the *Ahnenerbe* has been looking into it. Officially these scientists are working on long-range weather predictions; in fact, though, they are seeking to prove the cosmic-ice theory once and for all.

It sounds familiar. Atlantis . . . twins and dwarves. The *Ahnenerbe* is a department of the *Schutzstaffel*. *Schutzstaffel*: Defense Force. *Ahnenerbe*: Ancestral Heritage. It is from the *Ahnenerbe* that "Uncle Pepi" is sent his skulls and bones.

I am, of course, no stranger to feminine wiles. But I was disappointed, I was very disappointed, when the second night with Herta went no better than the first. Went no different, in fact. Will nothing "melt the ice"—the cosmic ice of marriage? The idea of a gradual familiarization was not without its initial appeal. But surely, I thought, on the third and final night, which we were to have all to ourselves . . .

Herta's nightdress is childish. It is patterned with genies and sprites. I begged of them, these sprites and genies. Deliriously, all night, in bed, I begged—oh, the bedbug of nightbeg . . . There were periods, earlier on, when I was calmer and we could talk a little. She spoke tearfully of *das Baby;* and the baby does sound fairly disastrous. I also got the distinct impression that Herta disapproves of the work I am doing here. In her incensed whisper she called me names I didn't understand. They made her face ugly, even in the dark. Why can't I answer?

The next day she was gone and the next night I was

back on the ramp. Playing Cupid. I still don't know what my wife looks like. She never met my eye. No. I never met hers. Things will improve. She will come around, in time. Has someone been telling her what I did to the bald whores?

Out on the ramp beneath the lights and the arrows of rain and the madhouse tannoy squawking *links* and *rechts:* fathers, mothers, children, the old, scattered like leaves in the wind. *Die . . . die Auseinandergeschrieben.* And I had a thought that made my whole body thrill with shame. Because the trains are endless and infernal, and because the wind feels like the wind of death, and because life is life (and love is love) but no one said it was easy.

I thought: It's all right for some.

With the war going so well now, and with the perceptible decline in the workload after the feats of '44, and with the general burgeoning of confidence and well-being, why, your camp doctor is agreeably surprised to find time and leisure to pursue his hobbies. The troglodytic Soviets have been driven back into their frozen potholes: the camp doctor steadies his monocle and reaches for his mustiest textbook. Or his binoculars and shooting stick. Whatever. Depending on natural bent. Winter was cold but autumn is come—the stubble fields, and so on. The simpering Vistula. Never before have I seen lice by the bushel. Some of the patients look as though they have been showered with poppy seeds. Good morning to you, *Scheissminister!* In one of her baffling letters Herta goes so far as to question the *legality* of the work we are doing here. Well. Let me see . . . I suppose you could say that there are one or two "gray areas." Block 11, the Black Wall, the measures of the Political Unit: these excite lively controversy. And there's certainly no end of a palaver when a patient "takes matters into his own hands,"

with the electrified fence, for example. We all *hate* that . . .
I am famed for my quiet dedication. The other doctors disappear for weeks on end; but in the summer air of the Kat-
Zet I have no need of *Sommerfrische*. I do love the feel of the
sun on my face, it's true. "Uncle Pepi" has surpassed himself
with his new laboratory: the marble table, the nickel taps,
the bloodstained porcelain sinks. Provincial: *that's* the word
for Herta. You know, of course, that she doesn't shave her
legs? It's true. About the armpits one can eternally argue,
but the legs—surely!—the legs . . . In this new lab of his
he can knock together a human being out of the unlikeliest
odds and ends. On his desk he had a box full of eyes. It
was not uncommon to see him slipping out of his darkroom
carrying a head partly wrapped in old newspaper: evidently,
we now rule Rome. The next thing you knew, there'd be,
oh, I don't know, a fifteen-year-old Pole sliding off the table
and rubbing his eyes and sauntering back to work, accompanied by an orderly and his understanding smile. We measure
twins together, "Uncle Pepi" and I, for hours and hours:
measure measure measure. Even the most skeletal patients
thrust their chests out for medical inspection in the last block
on the right: a scant fifteen minutes earlier they were flat on
the floor of the *Inhalationsraume*. It would be criminal—it
would be criminal to *neglect* the opportunity that Auschwitz
affords for the furtherance . . . I see him at the wheel of his
Mercedes-Benz, on the day the gypsy camp was established,
personally ferrying the children from "the central hospital."
The gypsy camp, its rosy pinks, its dirty prettiness. " 'Uncle
Pepi'!" " 'Uncle Pepi'!" the children cried. When was that?
When did we do the gypsy camp? Before the Czech family
camp? Yes. Oh, long ago. Herta came again. Her second
visit could not be accounted a complete success, though we
were much more intimate than before, and wept a lot

together about the baby. As to the so-called "experimental" operations of "Uncle Pepi": *he* had a success rate that approached—and quite possibly attained—100 percent. A shockingly inflamed eyeball at once rectified by a single injection. Innumerable ovaries and testes seamlessly grafted into place. Women went out of that lab looking twenty years younger. We can make another baby, Herta and I. If I wept copiously both before and after, she let me do it, or try it, but I am impotent and don't even go to the whores anymore. I have no power. I am completely helpless. The sweet smell here, the sweet smell, and the dazzled Jews. "Uncle Pepi" never left any scars. You know, it isn't all sweetness and light here, not by any manner of means. *Some of the patients were doctors.* And it wasn't long before they were up to their old tricks. I am prominent in the campaign against this filth. The baby will be here soon and I feel very concerned. "Uncle Pepi" is right: I do need a holiday. But my visit to Berlin for the funeral turns out be mercifully brief: I only remember the drizzling parquetry of the streets, the shop-lights like the valves of an old radio, the drenched church-yard, the skin and weight problems of the young cleric, Herta's parents, Herta's hideous face. There is a war on, I keep telling everyone. We are in the front line. What are we fighting? Phenol? On my return from Berlin to the light and space of the KZ, what should await me but a telegram. The baby is very weak, and the doctors have done all they can. The casket was about fifteen by twenty inches. I am fighting the phenol war, and thanklessly. No one shows me any gratitude. I seem to have developed a respiratory difficulty— stress asthma, perhaps—particularly when I am shouting. I have to shout. The pits are bursting. In the Sprinkleroom, when the guards touch the young girls, and I repeatedly register my objections, the men mime the playing of violins.

They think, because I am now a husband and father, that I have become pious and mawkish. I long to see my little Eva, of course; the present situation, however, is counterindicative. I have stopped going to the bordello but at least I now know why I went: for the gratitude. Those patient-doctors are getting quite out of hand. For some reason they are especially zealous in their interference with the children: how repulsive and wanton this is, when you consider that the children, after all, won't be around for very long. I am not "in it" for the gratitude. No. I am "in it"—if you want a *why*—because I love the human body and all living things. It isn't just phenol we're fighting, not anymore. In that sense the war front has widened. It is a war on death that now comes in many forms. As well as phenol we are obliged to extract prussic acid and sodium evipan. Time is running out. We have lost two Sprinklerooms. There is a tickling in the heart when completion is so near and there are souls still stacked like desperate airplanes circling above an airport. Some exceptions should be duly noted: an old man hugging and kissing my black boots; a child clinging to me after I held her down for "Uncle Pepi." But *not once* did I receive what might be described as sober and reasoned thanks. Oh, I'm not complaining. But it would have been nice. "Uncle Pepi," who used to thank me, disappeared months ago, leaving me to my own devices. I loved the man. As well as prussic acid and sodium evipan I now extract benzene, gasoline, kerosene, and air. Yes, air! Human beings want to be alive. They are dying to be alive. Twenty cubic centimeters of air—twenty cubic centimeters of nothing—is all you need to make the difference. So nobody thanks me as, with a hypodermic almost the size of a trombone and my right foot firmly stamped on the patient's chest, I continue to prosecute the war against nothing and air.

6

Multiply zero by zero and you still get zero

Well, how do you follow that?

The answer is: you can't. Of

course you can't.

And there comes a point where you have to call an end or at least announce a limit to sacrifice. Ah, I'm no saint, God knows. I wasn't put here just to live for others. And while I continued to make my contribution, I really did feel it was high time I started looking out for number one.

I followed the Kat-Zet with robust activity, with the wry observances of married life, and with emotion. This new thing in my life called emotion. My departure from Auschwitz I think of as *the wrench*. It never crossed my mind that I would ever recover from the suffering I underwent during my last days there, and especially my last hours. But it passed, quicker than any marsh fever, as I set out on my journey to Berlin—and was replaced by emotion, by the accession of innumerable sensitivities, not without their pivotal elements of pain. It was the pain, perhaps, of being young. It was 1942. I was twenty-five. . . . The train to Berlin, by the way, was prompt and expeditious. Auschwitz Central was no mere spur or siding. It was the biggest station I have ever seen, and served all Europe, direct. One of our last shipments went straight to Paris: Special Train 767, to Bourget-Drancy. Auschwitz was a secret. It covered fourteen thousand acres, and it was invisible. It was there, and it wasn't there. It was outside. So how can you follow it?

Herta is utterly transformed. Yes, my wife is more or less unrecognizable in every way. She *is* pregnant, after all— prodigious, luminous; and she pampers me outrageously. I don't quite know what I did to deserve this radical revision in status. Our German baby is of startling dimensions: bigger, if anything, than the woman herself. Herta is no more than the string on the parcel in which the baby sleeps. For the time being we reside with her parents in their small but practical house in the southern suburbs of Berlin. Much of our time is spent in morbid speculation about the baby's name. We favored Eva or Dieter at first; but now we seem to have settled on Birgitta or Eduard. Sensibly, if laboriously, Herta is dismantling the baby's clothes. I myself spend an hour or two a day in the garden hut with my father-in-law, dismantling the baby's cot and high chair. Our room, Herta's room, seems to be analogously prepared for her own eventual childhood. The fairies of the wallpaper smile down on the conjugal bed, which is a single, as slim as a bunk. Its dairy aroma encloses Herta, her shocking new breasts, her ovoid belly. The baby comes between us. It's more comfortable if Herta lies on her side and I take up position behind her. Annoyingly, however, I am still impotent. Nervous exhaustion, no doubt; perhaps, too, a guilty reminder (in the way our bodies are juxtaposed) of the gratitude I sampled in the camp. Though Herta has hair: lots of hair. Anyway, she talked to her doctor about it, unbearably, and he says that this is quite a common male reaction to pregnancy. Yes, either that, or it's the work I've been doing.

And continued to do. Oh, you know how it is. You say: Enough with these busybodies and goody two-shoes! And then you're out there again, doing what you can. After my fortnight's leave I completed a five-month tour of duty in the East with a Waffen SS unit, operating downwind, as it were, of the military withdrawal from the Soviet Union. I like to think we achieved a good deal, though it was humble stuff compared to the Kat-Zet. And crude stuff. And aesthetically catastrophic stuff too, of course. Emotion flits around me now. The world continues to make sense, but emotion isn't so interested in sense, and wonders how things feel. . . . My face, during this time, can best be imagined as a study in strain. Rather as it looked when I lay there in the dark, wedged between the changed Herta and the cold wall, in full confidence of erotic failure. Then it happens—

it doesn't happen—and you switch on the light and get dressed sadly. The sadness is your very own; it entirely fits you. And Herta's glance sometimes, and her mother's glance, and even her father's glance, which is hard and countervailing, which is on my side (but I don't want it): these glances say that in my hands there rests a mortal and miserable power. I am omnipotent. Also impotent. I am powerful and powerless.

It was a summer of thunder and sunshine and double rainbows. These were epiphanies. I finally encountered the bomb baby, thus fulfilling the ironic prophecy of my dreams. And with my own eyes I saw the stalled clock at Treblinka. . . .

What the unit was doing could, I suppose, be seen as a natural continuation of my work in the Lager. We were on the interface of bureaucracy and public relations. At this point the Jews were being deconcentrated, were being channeled back into society, and it fell to us to help dismantle and disperse the ghettos, where the light was always failing and where the children all looked so old and full of knowledge, and everybody moved much too slowly or much too fast. Even as an interim measure, the ghettos, one felt, were a failure, and made one suspect, briefly yet sickeningly, that the whole enterprise, the whole dream, had been fatally grandiose: too many, too many. How one longed to uproot those walls. . . . One ghetto, that of Litzmannstadt, had a "king": Chaim Rumkowski. I myself saw him parading through the stunned streets, with courtiers, in his carriage, pushed by a white horse like a paper bag full of water and bones. Rumkowski was a lord. But a lord of what?

Well, we pitched in, ferrying the people back to their villages and so on. Logistics. But the work also had its creative dimension. We used vans, vans marked with the Red

Cross; and machine guns; and dynamite. I turned out to have a modest talent for neuropsychiatry. The men to whom I gave counseling (and prescribed sedatives) would, for a while, complain of nightmares, anxiety, and dyspepsia—but they all recovered by the end of the tour. The measures to which we were sometimes reduced were distressingly inelegant, and, in those cases where dynamite was used, required hours of backbreaking preparation. But this was our mission, after all: to make Germany whole. To heal her wounds and make her whole.

One morning of diagonal sleet and frozen puddles we were unloading some Jewish families at a rude hamlet on the River Bug. It was the usual sequence: we'd picked up this batch from the mass grave, in the woods, and stood waiting by the van on the approach road while the carbon monoxide went about its work. All my men were dressed as doctors, with their white smocks, their dangling stethoscopes, their talk and their laughter and their cigarettes, waiting for the familiar volley of shouts and thumps from within. I myself toyed with a philosophical perfecto. . . . We then drove them closer to town, where one of our men was readying the piles of clothes. Out they all filed. Among them was a mother and a baby, both naked, naturally, for now. The baby was weeping in a determined, muscular, long-haul rhythm, probably from earache. Its mother already looked exasperated by these cries. Indeed she looked stunned— stopped dead in the face. For a moment I wondered if she'd fully come round from the carbon monoxide. I was concerned.

We then escorted this group of about thirty souls into a low warehouse littered with primitive sewing machines and spindles and bolts of cloth. Normally, now, one would have to chivy them off into their cellars and outhouses. But these

Jews, led by the weeping baby, made their solemn way past a series of curtains and blankets suspended from the ceiling and, one by one, backed their way through a missing panel in the wall. This panel I myself replaced with a softly spoken "Guten Tag." I don't know. I was moved, by their continued silence, by the baby's muffled cries. *"Raus! Raus!"* I shouted—to the men, who romped off to explore the premises, and to lay out some trinkets, and some food, some bread and tomatoes, say, as was traditional, for the Jews' later use. *"Raus! Raus! Raus!"* But I remained alone in the still warehouse, crouched by the wall, and listening. Listening? To the baby's weeping, and to the sound that perhaps the whole planet makes when it tries to soothe: "Schh . . . Schh." Hush now. I tiptoed away, and joined the men. Quiet. Best to leave them to it. Schh. This may be the way they soothe their young. Thirty souls in the black gap, saying Schh . . . The baby, then, was clearly much loved. But of course it had no power at all.

Finally Treblinka, on which we paid a brief courtesy call as we journeyed homeward through northern Poland to the Reich. This place too was already half-dismantled, its work done. As with Auschwitz, no memorial would mark the spot. But I wasn't too late. I got to see the famous "railway station"—which was a prop, a facade. Looked at sideways on, it rose like a splint into the winter sky. The idea was, of course, to reassure the Jews—the Jews of Warsaw, Radom, and the Bialystok districts whom the camp had serviced. There were signs and so on, saying, Restaurant and Ticket Office and Telephone, and informing passengers where to change for their onward journey, and a clock. Every station, every journey, needs a clock. When we passed it, on our way to inspect the gravel pits, the big hand was on twelve and the little hand was on four. Which was incorrect! An error, a mistake: it was exactly 13:27. But we passed again, later, and the hands hadn't moved to an earlier time. How could they move? They were painted, and would never move to an earlier time. Beneath the clock was an enormous arrow, on which was printed: Change Here For Eastern Trains. But time had no arrow, not here.

Indeed, at the railway station in Treblinka, the four dimensions were intriguingly disposed. A place without depth. And a place without time.

Herta continues to be very good, or at least very silent, about my impotence. After my tour, I didn't expect to hit top form right away. But this is ridiculous. It seems that the work I do takes so much of what is essential in me that there is nothing left. Nothing for Herta. In that sense I suppose I am making the ultimate sacrifice. During the counseling sessions some of the young troopers in the East mentioned impotence as being chief among their difficulties. My position there was simple: I told them not to worry about it. And that was a joke, because I was half-dead with worry myself. The bit of me, that is to say, that wasn't dead already: from impotence. Yes, most amusing, telling them they have to be hard (*harte*), that they have to be men (*Menschen*). And there you are, facing each other, two soggy zeros. Multiply zero, or anything else, by zero, and you still get zero. Furthermore, I've been doing my sums in another area and generally putting two and two together, and I figure that something has to happen before I'm reposted—to account for the baby. Our baby is a bomb, too: a time bomb. And if *I* don't do it . . . Herta's belly has gone down now. I am no longer obliged to lurk limply behind her. These days I get to lurk limply on top of her. By my absence I am conspicuous. We don't talk about it anymore, thank God. But I'm assuming it's still noticed.

The act of love did happen—and only once, and only

just—immediately before I took up my new post at Schloss Hartheim, near Linz, in the province of Austria. Real last-gasp stuff: it happened in the eye of a storm of tears that the whole house must have heard with horror. I was still crying when I put on my boots and picked up my kit bag; and after a few desperate embraces I burst out into the stars and the snow—the constellations of snow, the blizzard of stars.

With its noble grounds, its archways and courtyards, Schloss Hartheim—an hour from Linz, toward Eferding—looked fair to provide the ideal setting for my full recuperation. This Renaissance castle had until recently served as a children's home. And when you sat, trembling forgetfully, on one of the benches in the frosted gardens, with the grass like white hair standing on end, you felt you could hear the ghosts of the children's cries and shouts—for here they must surely have played in their packs. Behind you stood the tall windows, in fives, and the glimpsed interiors always the color of watery gravy. A bucket, a mop; an orderly in his white coat; a patient's illegible gaze. That smell again. The sweet smell . . . Now I lean forward and pick up a dead bird whose wings sag open like a fan or like the streets of Berlin under their cam nets. Berlin, where Herta waits.

Considered as an institutional bridge, Schloss Hartheim was part of my winding down from the experience of the KZ. Apart from obvious differences in scale, there were close analogies. You found the same collegial spirit, with its masonic taciturnity and instinctive discretion, the same camaraderie and grit, the same alcohol reliance. I am positioned between the two chief medical officers and the fourteen nurses, seven male, seven female. This is not a convalescent home: no patient ever spends the night. Here comes the bus with its tinted windows. It surges up into the grounds of the fabled castle, into the cold and weary magic of Schloss Hartheim.

It went like this, the sequence. Step one saw the arrival of a regulation urn of ashes, sent to us direct by the patient's family, who would also notify the Condolence-Letter Department in Berlin, with whom we worked in parallel. These ashes, in their small portions, were accompanied by the death certificates of distinct individuals; but ashes are just ashes, and they all look the same, and they went straight into the pot of the Hartheim incinerator. What was wrong? What was the matter? Were the ovens malfunctioning? Was the Chamber faulty? Because the people we produced just weren't any good anymore. All the wizardry and delirium, all the insomnia and diarrhea of Auschwitz—it was failing. Yes, that's right: the wards, the examination rooms, the silent gardens of Schloss Hartheim were heavy with a sense of failing magic. At first the patients really weren't that bad. Some little defect. Clubfoot. Cleft palate. But later they were absolutely hopeless. I try not to look at them closely, the patients, as I lead them in their paper bibs from the Chamber; I keep visualizing my own viscera, and there is something solid and man-made in there, like a lead pipe, snagged and dragging. Here, the gentle hesitancy of the blind. There, the lopsided, the scalene visage of the deaf. The white-haired lady looks nice but everything is wrong. The mad boy screams as he chases the male nurses down the damp corridors. The mad girl crouching in the corner with her frock up and the unforgivable substance coming from her mouth. There is such a thing, we say here, as life that is unworthy of life, and I don't know about that, but nobody wants them, not even us, and they leave here the same day for some other place, in the coach with the tinted windows.

Herta comes down to visit me as often as she can, which is not very often, because this is wartime, after all. We stay at the Gasthaus Drei Krönen on the Landstrasse near Linz, where I am impotent, and once we had a romantic weekend at the Hotel Gretchen in Vienna, where I was impotent. There is a small officers' annex in the village itself for me to be impotent at, and it is on this hygienic apartment that we increasingly depend. As time goes by, Herta seems more and more put out—by my impotence. She says I've changed but I don't think that's true. I've been impotent for as long as I can remember. She also upbraids me about the work I am engaged in at Schloss Hartheim. There are rumors in the village, there is gossip—latrine talk. She has got it all wrong, but then, too, I pooh-pooh her less grandly than I might. We hold hands across the table in the coffee shop. We part. Later in the dusk I entertain a perplexed perfecto as I walk back up the hill to the castle, to Schloss Hartheim. Above its archways and gables the evening sky is full of our unmentionable mistakes, hydrocephalic clouds and the wrongly curved palate of the west, and the cinders of our fires. I can see a lock of snow-white human hair drifting upward, then joining the more elliptical and elemental rhythm of the middle air. Tonight there'll be a party in the basement at the Schloss to mark the arrival of our five thousandth patient (though I'm sure we've had many, many more than that), with Manfred on accordion: songs, toasts, pink party hats. Christian Wirth, our roving director, will be there: his belly, his colorful language, his exploded drinker's face. Patient Five Thousand will also be present, in paper hat (and paper shirt), suspended in its journey between fire and gas, awaiting its span of deformity, hallucination, and constant itching. . . . He walks on, alone, Odilo Unverdorben.

Fully alone.

I who have no name and no body—I have slipped out from under him and am now scattered above like flakes of ash-blonde human hair. No longer can I bear with the ruined god, betrayed and beaten by his own magic. Calling on powers best left unsummoned, he took human beings apart—and then he put them back together again. For a while it worked (there was redemption); and while it worked he and I were one, on the banks of the Vistula. He put *us* back together. But of course you shouldn't be doing any of this kind of thing with human beings. . . . The party is over. He lies there in the peeling pyramid of the attic bedroom, on his cot shaped like a gutter. A damp pink pillow is twisted in his fists. I'll always be here. But he's on his own.

7

She loves me, she loves me not

The world has stopped making sense again, and Odilo forgets everything again (which is probably just as well), and the war is over now (and it seems pretty clear to me that we lost it), and life goes on for a little while.

Odilo is innocent. His dreams are innocent, purged of menace and sickness. Oh, sure, he quivers on slippery poles as tall as the moon is high, and lopes nude down tunnels while alarm clocks sound, etc.—but there are no worrying resonances. And, as against that, his sleep savors many vulgar triumphs with treasure chests and locks of hair and sleeping beauties. And toilet bowls. The tutelary spirit of these dreams is no longer the man in the white coat and the black boots: it is a woman, a woman the size and shape of a galleon's sail, who can forgive him everything. My hunch is that this woman is his mother, and I'm anxious to know when she's going to show up. Odilo is innocent. Odilo is, it turns out, innocent, emotional, popular, and stupid.

Also potent. He has no power whatever, of course, and does his stuff in the Reserve Medical Corps with impeccable ovinity. But he's potent. Ask little Herta, who will defeatedly attest to it. She can barely walk. National Socialism is nothing more than applied biology. Odilo is a doctor: a biological soldier. So this two-year orgy we're having must form part of his personal campaign. He's on active service; he smells powder; he's going over the top for the baby. Yes, they still want one, even though Eva was such a disappointment. When Odilo has Herta on the bed, splayed and buckled, with her ankles on either side of the headboard, it's as if he's trying to kill something rather than create it. But we all know by now that violence creates, here on earth. Never before have we been so potent, not even in New York when we were combing nurses out of our hair. Herta sometimes looks as though she could do with the odd impotent interlude. But there aren't any. What made the difference, I wonder? After Schloss Hartheim, which seemed to go on forever, the three of us moved out of her parents' house and came down here to Munich and its Alpine air. Away from

Herta's childhood room, away from the angels on the walls that used to watch over her. Here, in our apartment, we have a skeleton watching over us, made of white wood, and anatomical drawings loud with ginger meat.

The German girl is a natural girl. She comes just as she is. With no makeup and hairy legs. This is okay by Odilo. In fact he forbids the use of cosmetics, even soap; and as for her hair and down, her crackling armpits, her upper locks and lower wreath—Herta, I suspect, could be woollier than any yak and still keep Odilo happy. He calls her his *Schimpanse:* his chimpanzee. I have to say that I'm mad about her too. Herta's body gossips with youth. Her ears are like cookies, her teeth are like candy. Her flesh is as taut as the flesh of an olive. At first she wasn't so keen, always complaining of tiredness or soreness or emotional unease; but these days, as Odilo says again and again to all his friends (and the compliment, I think, is pitched decorously high), she bangs like a shithouse door in a gale. Herta is so small that it seems natural to be quite strict with her. She is eighteen. And getting smaller all the time. One mustn't give in to pessimism, and it's pointless to look too far ahead, but in a couple of years she won't even be legal.

It's very sweet. Now that the wedding nears, Odilo is altogether gentler. He has stopped having tantrums. No longer is his chimpanzee required to do the housework naked, and on all fours. Herta responds with gratitude, and with an apparently unbounded tenderness, never seen before. . . . Erotic rapture, it transpires, is in a sense a reptilian condition. The higher mind, the soul, the princes of the faculties—they absent themselves. And so, too, most emphatically, does the reptile brain. Let me think about it. When reptile brains get together, they want to do harm from a position of safety. But when it's just their bodies, they seem to want to do good, and close up, with maximum risk to the self. I don't know. I'm still there, in their bed, and I like it; but the oozy ecstasy belongs to Odilo, that glistening lizard, and to Herta, that glistening lizardess, in their world of succulent slime, where no words are necessary: you just croak and hum. . . . Their love life is steadily divesting itself of all irregularities. For instance, they used to play a kind of game (about twice a week, or rather more often if Odilo put his foot down), where she must lie still and show no sign of life, throughout. Similarly, he used to take a healthy interest in his wife's bowel movements, as is meet. But that's all behind him now. When she weeps and sulks, he dries her tears with kisses, and not with a punch in the breasts. And nowadays she hardly cries at all: the wedding is only weeks away. Less and less often, though still pretty regularly (say most nights), Odilo quits his pact of reptiles and, with enthusiasm, seeks his herds of friends: their strength in musky numbers, their heat of hide and stall. We shout and we drool, with the distorted faces of babies; individually we have no power or courage, but together we form a glowing mass. Often the night's play begins with us going out and helping Jews. Odilo, Herta, and I are officially on our honeymoon now but in fact we're going nowhere. Except back to Berlin, for the wedding.

My position on the Jews has always been without ambiguity. I like them. I am, I would say, one of nature's philo-Semites. It's their eyes I particularly admire. That glossy, heated look. An exoticism that points toward the transcendent—who knows? Anyway, why talk about their *qualities?* I am childless; but the Jews are my children and I love them as a parent should, which is to say that I don't love them for their qualities (remarkable as these seem to me to be, naturally), and only wish them to exist, and to flourish, and to have their right to life and love.

I remember names and faces, names I heard called at dawn gatherings in town squares, or by empty fuel pits and antitank ditches, or under the light of policemen's bonfires, or in waiting zones, in train stations, in green fields at night. And names I saw on printed lists, quotas, manifests. Lonka and Mania, and Zonka and Netka, Liebish, Feigele, Aizik, Yaacov, Motl, and Matla, and Zipora, and Margalit. Back from Auschwitz-Birkenau-Monowitz, from Ravens-bruck, Sachsenhausen, Natzweiler and Theresienstadt, from Buchenwald and Belsen and Majdanek, from Belzec, from Chelmno, from Treblinka, from Sobibor.

The sick smile that Odilo sported throughout his wedding day seems, in retrospect, all too appropriate. I kept seeing this leer of his, the leer of a wary yokel, reflected in the numerous little mirrors set around Herta's marriage crown (traditional: to ward off evil spirits, and so on). Yes, his smile was a good commentary on the occasion; ditto the painfully explosive backslaps delivered by his many new men friends. How else should a person look, while, in the course of a single ceremony, he kisses everything goodbye—just blows it all away in a prodigal storm of confetti and rice? She gave me the wreath of myrtle, the saffron and cinnamon, the bread, the butter, and the rest of it. And I gave her all my power. We switched our rings from the fourth finger of the left hand to the fourth finger of the right. They said it was an auspicious marriage moon: it was rising. But I could see that the moon above my head was really on the wane. Hence the unbearable blows to back and shoulder. Hence the coprophagic smile. Hence Herta's triumphal laughter.

She delightedly moves back into her parents' house, and lies there, among golden-winged angels. And Odilo? Where are *our* parents, for Christ's sake? Suddenly I'm in a five-floor boardinghouse, turbid with cabbage and gym shoes, sharing an attic with Rolf and Reinhard and Rüdiger and Rudolph, and living a nightmare, an *Alpdruck*, of towel fights and textbooks and jokes about courtship and corpses. That's right: I'm at med school. In the New Germany too, and feeling rather jumpy and furtive along with everybody else. Even the streets are like a dorm these days, with much peer-group pressure and unpredictably intense scrutiny, adolescent, unpleasant, sexual but sexually obscure or half-formed, and made up of ridiculous postures no one is allowed to laugh at. Laugh at these ridiculous postures, and everybody will want to kill you. How fortunate that I am unkillable. Unkillable, but not immortal. What happened to our manhood?

It could be worse, because we still see Herta every day, at the school: she's a tight-skirted secretary in Superintendence. I often get ten minutes with her in a corridor, and sit quite near her table in the cafeteria, and there's a stairwell where we go and kiss—where we breathe into one another. Apart from that it's park benches and dark archways. Mickey Mouse sniggers and Greta Garbo averts her pained gaze from our mortified writhings on the shallow fur of cinema seats. We cling close in the safety of crowds under streetlights and torchlights. During certain ten-minute intervals in her parents' front room, while they set out the filthy plates for dinner, I have achieved much . . . Also on our spring and summer picnics. Among the delphinium, the snapdragon, the hollyhock, and the sweet pea, on a blanket, by a basket, she will grant me a nostalgic caress—always followed, on Odilo's part, by hours of sniveling entreaty. Where once we ruled, now we serve. His most prosperous theme is that the frustration is damaging his health. Another thing that usually works is the naming of flowers, in English. The woods embolden her. The German girl is a natural girl. Odilo is hysterically grateful for any sylvan handful or eyeful or mouthful that comes his way. But I'm not. He forgets. I remember. This tormented groping. I am excoriated by erotic revanchism. And I know something he seems unable to face: it will never happen again. The future always comes true. Sadly we gather forget-me-nots. She loves me. . . . Actually we hardly dare look at her now, the tiny typist, such power does she wield. *Ja* say the ghosts of painted letters on the trees in the avenues. *Nein* says Herta as she takes my hand and places it, for an angry moment, between her thighs. Then, in the late afternoon, to the school: zygoma, xanthelasma, volvulus, all drained from him, at least, at last, all that ugly shit. But most of his lessons, to my surprise, aren't about the human body being a machine: they are about hospital administration. Sometimes, late at night, Odilo and I sneak out alone onto the roof of the board- inghouse, while the Germans dream their dreams. There we enjoy a precocious (and faintly paranoid) perfecto, and watch the stars, which seem to soothe our sight.

A parallel pleasure and comfort, for me at any rate, was to watch the Jews. The people I had helped to dream down from the heavens. And I was inspired by the size of the contribution they were clearly destined to make. It would all work out. Wisely cautious at first—awed, probably, by sheer numbers (because they were coming in, now, from all over the shop, from Canada, from Palestine)—German soci- ety duly broadened itself to let the newcomers in. Their brisk assimilation, and their steady success, caused some harsh words to be spoken. The Jews were walking into all the plum jobs, in the medical profession especially, which infuriated Odilo and his friends, and which, to be frank, even worried me. I hadn't come all this way to see my sons turn into *doctors*. But what the hell. Somebody's got to do it: for some reason. Despite my worsening cares and loneliness, the racial-law repeals always rallied me. Even here, though, there was a sadistic irony at work, because these progressive measures always coincided with some fresh interdiction of Herta's. Yes, very droll, no doubt. With step after step the Jews move blinking into the sunlight. While I am gradually declassed: mocked and spurned by all the liberties of love. For example.

Blind and deaf Jews can now wear armbands identifying their condition in traffic. I no longer have a lower body, an external heart, in Herta's scheme of brings. I am cut off at the waist forever.

Jews allowed to keep pets; budgies and puppies, etc., doled out at police stations; Jews weeping with gratitude as they take their new playmates home. Herta starts to breathe differently as we kiss; she is always self-possessed; every move of mine is coldly monitored.

Jews permitted to buy meat, cheese, and eggs. Revocation of all picnicking privileges, even though I whine about my health and name flowers in English until I'm blue in the face.

Jews empowered to have friendly relations with Aryans. Herta no longer says "I love you." I still say it. Kissing continues, after a fashion, but tongues now completely verboten.

Curfew for Jews lifted. It used to be nine P.M. in summer and eight P.M. in winter. Herta has to be home by eight-thirty, whatever the season.

The designation Unbeliever ceases to be mandatory for the Jews. But I have to say that I no longer believe.

She loves me, she loves me not. I take the same two-hour bus and tram ride for the same old peck on the cheek. Soon she will celebrate her sixteenth birthday. Then what?

156

Will we even hold hands? Sometimes, wildly, I find myself urging Odilo to use violence (quickly, before she's fifteen): violence, which mends and heals. Actually, though, I have little enthusiasm for the venture. Could he do it, do you think? Is it in him? I've come to the conclusion that Odilo Unverdorben, as a moral being, is absolutely unexceptional, liable to do what everybody else does, good or bad, with no limit, once under the cover of numbers. He could never be an exception; he is dependent on the health of his society, needing the sandy smiles of Rolf and Rudolph, of Rüdiger, of Reinhard. On Kristallnacht when we all romped and played and helped the Jews, and the fizzy shards swirled like stars or souls, and when Herta bent to wipe her lips with a pink handkerchief—before spitting my tongue out of her mouth. Is it somehow the Jews' fault? That lock of her hair he had, kept in a pillbox—why did he return it? Now I can exactly see the shape and size, the perfect fit, of the loneliness that is approaching. She gives me flowers, but she loves me not. She loves me not.

Still, sprich durch die Blume. Hush now, speak through a flower. I know you shouldn't grumble: for one thing, it's against the law. . . . She's stopped talking to me. It was only a matter of time. Hush now. One day at the bus stop, as she alighted, she just waved goodbye to me. In the evenings I still wait there for her, and track her as she walks to school, with my ears humming. Now she moves right through my gaze, which no longer has the power to slow or halt her. Then she vanished. Her small shape is gone, forever, replaced by a void of the same dimensions. I look for her everywhere—but *he* doesn't. Odilo's recovery was idiotically swift. The very next day he was upbraided by the professor for giggling out loud in Gross Anatomy: Rolf and Rudolph were making jokes about the new female corpse. Indeed, his affections seem to have redirected themselves, platonically but otherwise intact, to fair-browed Reinhard. . . . I suffer alone. *Arzt für Seelisches Leiden,* say the placards in the ground-floor windows. Doctor for sick souls. Now that sounds like the kind of doctor I need. At present we're spending much of our time at the hospital, as a visitor— because our mother's turned up at last. Her name, by the way, is Margaret. Odilo and I have been airing the new apartment until it is heavy with her smell. I suppose we'll probably set up house together. At least she'll be someone to talk to. In English. She reminds me of Irene. She keeps saying, "Where am I? Where am I?" "In the hospital," Odilo keeps dourly replying. "In the hospital. In the ward in the hospital. *Das Krankenhaus, Mutti. Im Krankenhaus.*"

In the *what?* I want to take her hand and say, Mother. You are on a globe that looks like a crystal ball or a marble in a light bed of cotton wool. Birds fly around it. Mother, you are on the planet earth.

Part III

8

Because ducks are fat

Ever since my days at Schloss Hart-

heim I had thought of making a

sentimental journey, to Auschwitz.

The place of power on the confluence of the rivers; the place where the numbered Jews, and all the others, who had no number, came down from the heavens; the place where, for a time, there was no why. And it happened. In 1929. I had done a fair bit of traveling by then, during my military service and my labor service and my Strength Through Joy holidays and all the rest of it, and I thought I'd missed my chance. But it happened. I was thirteen.

It happened on a camping trip sponsored by one of the youth organizations that derived from the old *Stalhhelm*. The morning was colorless with fog when we bivouacked on the left bank of the Sola. I unrolled my sleeping bag, quite unthinkingly, though I noticed the patches of arrow grass, the familiar three-pronged marsh plant, with its burst points. That night the arrow grass filled me with inklings, and disquieted me, as Odilo slept. When I awoke, the air was warm and the night was clear beneath the deep and uncrackable code of the stars. We sat around the fire, as you do, and sang and chanted and yodeled; then I picked up the buckets and went with Dieter, whom Odilo loved, to bring water to the shallows. And there it was: the confluence of the rivers under a hunter's moon, and the railway tracks in their arrested journey.

Later we filed past the site. There were about twenty brick hovels, apparently held together by their own filth (Austrian artillery barracks, for the War), and, a little farther on, several ridiculously undistinguished buildings, which belonged, I learned, to the Polish Tobacco Monopoly. Oswiecim. Auschwitz. Beyond, through the birch wood, lay Birkenau: beyond, through the birch wood, lay birchy Birkenau, where I was in harmony with the engine of nature. Everything was miserable and innocent. All the quiddity, all the power and wonder, had been washed away by time and weather.

*   *   *

I'm three years old now and living, in rather reduced circumstances, on the southern edge of a town called Solingen.

Solingen is famous for its knives, its scissors, and its surgical instruments. From a catchment area that spans much of central Europe, the knives, the scissors, and the surgical instruments are gathered here in Solingen and turned into steel. Also, and quite nearby, we can offer golf, riding, tennis, and archery. Finally, modest Solingen harbors a proud secret. I'm the only one who happens to know what that secret is. It's this: Solingen is the birthplace of Adolf Eichmann. Schh . . . Hush now. I'll never tell. And if I did, who would believe me?

Soon I'll be born too. This terraced house will be my birthplace. It's a pretty tense situation, I suppose, but I don't let it get me down. In fact my lucid intervals are increasingly brief and rare. Father is a sallow-fleshed skeleton with half a right foot. Mother is like warm pastry in the icing of her nightdress. She is a nurse: she works in Solingen's Home for the Old. Odilo's days are fabulous drugs but we still need to cry sometimes until Father takes the pain away with a rhythmical upward sweep of his rattling hand. Then we are happy again (and up to no good). Mother's faith is intercessionary; but he has the power. The morning coos at Odilo and me in a language only we can hear. To our mother we say things like:

"Mummy? Chickens are alive. We catch them and burn them—and then they're dead! But you can't eat chicks. Not little good chicks. Because chicks are good. You can just stroke them and everything. But you *can* eat ducks. Because ducks are fat."

Wait. Mistake there. Mistake. Category . . . We brang. We putten. We brang, we putten, their own selves we tooken all away. Why so many children and babies? What got into us? Why so many? We were cruel: the children weren't even going to be here for very long. I choiced it, did I? Why? Because babies are fat? . . . But now we're away, running through the field where every living thing flourishes in desperate abandon, and lurching each second between joy and horror, our mind full of nonsensical objections to nonsensical premises, and ignorant and innocent, never having known anyone, even Irene, even Rosa, even Herta, even the Jews and the others I made.

Only Mother. Our relations are already very intimate and, if everything goes through okay, will soon get more intimate still. For instance, many, many hours of every day and night I shall spend cradled in her arms, kissing her breasts. (It will be allowed. He can't stop it.) Then eventually our corporeal bond will be tied, with Solingen scissors. When I enter her, how she will weep and scream. That I am gone. Odilo himself doesn't know how much power we have over her and how much she loves us: he doesn't sense her when she comes in the night and loosens our blankets and feels our brow and cries with worry when we're sick. . . . Soon, Father will have her all to himself. I think he is starving. He is as thin as a *Muselmann*. When he eats, he just doesn't come up with enough. Not enough—not enough to keep body and soul together. It is with an internal smirk that I call him *Fatti*. His furious, unforgiving, defeated look: his eyes are grimed with it, his face is nutcrackered with defeat and with unhealed wounds. He will probably improve, after the War. His ruined foot will improve. Naturally I cannot forgive my father for what he will have to do to me. He will come in and kill me with his body. Odilo knows this and feels this too.

I must make one last effort to be lucid, to be clear. What finally concerns me are questions of time: certain durations. Even as things stood, the Jews were made to wait too long in city squares, with their children getting difficult, and I now know how difficult they can get, when they start creating: how quickly their worlds can fall away. The Jews were made to wait too long in summer meadows, under racing skies, where families were often united by procedures that involved too much suspense, with children running this way and that and stopping still with their hands raised like claws, searching, and babies on the ground every few yards in shawls, crying, with no parents readily available, for much too long. . . . Now Odilo's dreams are all colors and noises, rapturous or dread filled, but with no content, not anymore.

He pauses for a moment, in the field. Only a moment. There are no larger units of his time. He has to act while childhood is still here, while everything is his playmate— including his *ca-ca*. He has to act while childhood is still here, before somebody comes and takes it away. And they will come. I hope the doctor will be wearing something nice, something appropriate, and not the white coat and the black boots, which surely . . . Myself. Mistake. Mistake. We brang, we putten. Look! Beyond, before the slope of pine, the lady archers are gathering with their targets and bows. Above, a failing-vision kind of light, with the sky fighting down its nausea. Its many nuances of nausea. When Odilo closes his eyes, I see an arrow fly—but wrongly. Point first. Oh no, but then . . . We're away once more, over the field. Odilo Unverdorben and his eager heart. And I within, who came at the wrong time—either too soon, or after it was all too late.

Afterword

This book is dedicated to my sister Sally, who, when she was very young, rendered me two profound services. She awakened my protective instincts; and she provided, if not my earliest childhood memory, then certainly my most charged and radiant. She was perhaps half an hour old at the time. I was four.

I also owe a great debt to my friend Robert Jay Lifton. Two summers ago I found myself considering the idea of telling the story of a man's life backward in time. Then, one afternoon, after a typically emotional encounter on the tennis court, Lifton gave me a copy of his book *The Nazi Doctors*. My novel would not and could not have been written without it. Probably the same applies to the works of Primo Levi, in particular *If This Is a Man*, *The Truce*, *The Drowned and the Saved*, and *Moments of Reprieve*. Other writers whom I found especially helpful, for various reasons, include Martin Gilbert, Gitta Sereny, Joachim Fest, Arno Mayer, Erich Fromm, Simon Wiesenthal, Henry Orenstein, and Nora Waln. At the back of my mind I also had a certain short story by Isaac Bashevis Singer and a certain paragraph—a famous one—by Kurt Vonnegut. (I won't list the authors of the medical textbooks I unenthusiastically pored over; but I am glad to thank Lawrence Shainberg for his entertaining and terrifying *Brain Surgeon*.) Then, too, one's feelings about this subject—here I mean the Holocaust—emerge and develop through conversation, over many years. I am grateful to my interlocutors, among them my wife, Antonia Phillips; my father, Kingsley Amis; my stepfather-in-law, Xan Fielding; my brother- and sister-in-law, Chaim and Susannah Tannenbaum; my brother-in-law, Matthew Spender; and Tom Maschler, Peter Foges, Piers and Emily Read, John Gross, Christopher Hitchens, James Fox, Zachary Leader, Clive James, Joseph Boothby, Sholom Globerman, Ian McEwan, Saul and Janis Bellow, Edmund and Natalia Fawcett, Jonathan Wilson, Michael Pietsch, and David Papineau.

My alternative title was *The Nature of the Offense*—a phrase of Primo Levi's. The offense was of such a nature that perhaps we can see Levi's suicide as an act of ironic heroism, an act that asserts something like: My life is mine and mine alone to take. The offense was unique, not in its cruelty, nor in its cowardice, but in its style—in its combination of the atavistic and the modern. It was, at once, reptilian and "logistical." And although the offense was not definingly German, its style was. The National Socialists found the core of the reptile brain, and built an autobahn that went there. Built for speed and safety, built to endure for a thousand years, the *Reichsautobahnen*, if you remember, were also designed to conform to the landscape, harmoniously, like a garden path.

M. A.
London
May 1991